DASH-

Life Between the Numbers

GREG ARMAMENTOS

Sourajit —

It is an honor and a pleasure to work with you. May you "dare greatly" and "strive valiantly" in all your interests and relationships.

Enjoy your dash!

Sincerely —

Mr. Armamento

ISBN #: 978-1-492-104773

Summary: As he nears the completion of junior high school, Dexter has his sights set on becoming famous for his running ability and speed. A serious illness, as well as unresolved family strife, raise obstacles to his pursuit and cause him to evaluate his goals.

The text type was set in 12-pt. Tahoma.

To Mary Kay, for co-writing our wonderful life story. To Rachel and Kelsey, who have always loved hearing, telling, and reading stories. To all three of you, I love being part of your story. To all those who have courageously walked through cancer – yours is a story of strength and dignity. Thank you for sharing it with us.

Table of Contents

Chapter 1

dash – (v): to throw or thrust violently or suddenly

Each day is a series of races. Racing to get out of bed when the alarm clock sounds in the morning. Or better yet, to beat the alarm. Racing to get in the shower before my sister takes the bathroom hostage with all of her hair-poofing and make-up painting. Racing to the school bus. Racing to get homework out of the way so I can get outside, and run.

At least my day is ending just the way it started – *running*. I woke up at 5:44 this morning, just moments before my alarm went off, and was out the door before my Dad's 5:50 buzzer sounded. In those initial few minutes, I had already won the first two races of the day – getting up before my alarm, and getting out the door before Dad's. Next up, was the process of triumphing over my toughest opponent – my ambition.

Already the fastest kid in my school, I have my eyes fixated on a couple of larger targets. First, is breaking the elusive four-minute mile. In our nation's history, there have only been four high school athletes to ever break the four-minute mile barrier. The fastest high-school mile is 3:53, set by Alan Webb of Virginia in 2001. A Google-search of Webb produces over 125,000 hits. Talk about a famous runner! To those of us who take running seriously, he is like the Babe Ruth of running – he seems out of our league. *For now.* I start high school next fall, and I aim to break Alan's record before I graduate.

The other target is a little bit harder to define. I probably won't know if I hit it until I am much older. Essentially, I want to do something so memorable, run a distance so fast, that my name will be its' own brand. Like Jordan. Gretzky. Tiger. Or perhaps my name will be synonymous with my accomplishment. Just the mere mention of a simple number will conjure up a glorious memory of how great I was. If an ardent baseball fan hears the number 56, what name comes to mind? Joe DiMaggio – known for his 56 game hitting streak. 61? People think of Roger

Maris – who clubbed 61 home runs in a single season (before the steroid era distorted everything). My personal favorite number in baseball is 130. Real aficionados know that the eternal speedster, Rickey Henderson, swiped 130 bases in 1982. In the sport of running, 4:00:00 is also a golden number, referring to the four-minute mile barrier that was long considered a sacred measure of running immortality. England's Roger Bannister was the first to ever record a mile dash in less than four minutes. Soon I hope to join that small group of elite immortals to crash that barrier.

So this morning I was at it again, running. This time I was training for next month's county track meet, aiming to beat last year's best time, and best runner – Dexter Allen Stevens-Hamilton. That's the tall, scrawny kid I notice in the mirror when I brush my teeth. Grandpa used to call me his "long drink of water". I think it was his kind way of saying I'm gangly. While being a beanpole might not garner me much attention from the hot girls in our school, (like the gorgeous Kelly Coughlin, sigh), it seems to be the perfect body type for my primary passion – running.

Last year I took first place in the middle school division of the county meet, beating my longtime nemesis Forrest Murphy in three separate events, as well as surpassing the best times posted by several high school students. Today I was up early training for the mile run, with a goal of finishing in under 4:20, and shaving 10 seconds off of my winning time from last year. At this rate, the sub-four-minute mile would be within my reach once I was in high school.

There is nothing quite like running. The cool, crisp morning air breezing across my skin. Friendly waves from neighbors out walking their dogs. The peaceful quiet of my thoughts, sometimes filled with dreaming about the next victory, and sometimes filled with absolutely nothing; just a freedom from having to think at all. This is my favorite part about running. Absolute freedom. Because sometimes thinking leads to memories. Sometimes I don't want to remember.

During the first quarter mile, I realized something was wrong. My pace was fine, but the rumbling in my tummy was more than a little annoying; it was painful. I knew I overdid it last night with that second PBJ. I was celebrating the "A" I had earned on my recent algebra test by fixing a second helping of my favorite sandwich, the PBJ (peanut butter and jalapenos). Maybe the jalapenos were bad. They did taste a bit more potent than normal. Other than a little extra gas last night, everything seemed fine. However, by the time I passed the three quarter mile mark and was preparing to go into my "kick" to the finish line, my stomach was screaming bloody murder. Determined to finish, I kept running until the PBJ's decided they had to be ejected immediately. It was the first time I had ever stopped running before reaching the finish line.

Halting on the Durham's front lawn, I began heaving up a jalapeno-muck-paste that burned worse on the way up than it had going down. Grandpa always warned me that those sandwiches would be the death of me. I was just wiping my mouth after the third heave when I noticed Kelly Coughlin across the street, stopped on her driveway, her silky blonde hair complimented by a teal tank top and lime green shorts, bent over the morning newspaper, witnessing the whole episode. Great. I had no idea she lived across from the Durham's. I'm such an idiot.

I finally dragged myself home, my training time wiped out and my coolness factor continuing to plummet. For a finale, as I entered the garage, my stomach felt the need to lurch one more time, right into dad's open toolbox. Ewww. Sorry Pops.

Dad helped me to the bathroom and called the school to let them know I was sick. He figured this must be more than spoiled jalapenos, and set up an appointment to get to the doctor later this morning. It was more likely the flu. Several kids had missed a few days of school recently, and I probably came in contact with whatever germs they were spreading. Perhaps I should be washing my hands before lunch period like some of those nerdy kids do. Oh well.

By the time we arrived at Dr. Mitchell's office, the vomiting had not yet ceased – it only changed in texture. No more jalapenos. I'm guessing whatever was left from the last few meals must have come up, too. Possibly even the remnants of the chocolate Easter bunny I snagged from my sister Kara's basket. Since she didn't seem in any hurry to finish it off, I pilfered the ears from her bunny as a little treat the other night before hitting the sack.

Dr. Mitchell ran a few tests, between my "episodes", and gave my dad a prescription to help settle my system and combat whatever flu bug I had. He sent me home to rest and recuperate, and I was so exhausted that Dad nearly had to carry me in from the car when we got home. After a few more hours of intermittent vomiting, my concerned father concluded that this was some serious bug, and decided to take me to the hospital. I've been here ever since.

Other than doctors, nurses, and parents delivering babies, everyone hates hospitals. Even the babies come out crying when they see this place. Hospitals creep me out. Sick people are everywhere. Patients amble ever so slowly. And you just know there are needles lurking around every corner. At least Dad is by my side. He is my rock.

The last time I was in a hospital, was the only time I was in one. Dad, and I suppose Mom, were here with me, doing whatever it is that parents do with their newborn children. As the story goes, they were certain of two things before I was born. Number One - that I was going to be a girl, even though they hadn't seen the results of the ultrasound test beforehand. They just had a gut feeling. Number Two – that I was going to be famous. I guess one out of two isn't so bad.

Parents have a funny way of settling all of these matters before birth. Dad always hoped to groom a child to be a runner, since next to teaching, running was his passion. Mom wanted to raise a musician, because she was a fairly accomplished saxophonist, and music was always the main love of her life. It still is. Apparently, they made some cockeyed deal that since the first child was going to be a girl, Mom would get to choose the name. If they ever had a son, then Dad would get to name him.

Well, when I came out, there was no doubt that their firstborn was indeed a *boy*, but Mom did not want to relinquish the chance to name her firstborn. Had I been a girl, I would have been named Claire, after her favorite saxophonist, Claire Daly. Since I was thankfully not stuck being a girl, I got stuck another way, with an unusual name – Dexter. Apparently Mom also adored some saxophonist named Dexter Gordon. I've never heard of him in any music class, but his name will forever haunt me.

It didn't take long, however, for the perfect nickname to take hold. I was born for speed. Everything I do, I do in turbo mode. Whether racing up and down stairs at home, being the first to complete my assignments at school (they really should give some type of prize for that), or absolutely loving to run – I was designed to fly. It wasn't long before my parents used my initials as a clever sounding moniker for me – Dexter Allen Stevens-Hamilton: "DASH". A perfect name for a famous runner. Could be some serious endorsement opportunities there.

I guess I owe Mom at least a little thanks for keeping her maiden name when she married Dad. Otherwise I would have been Dexter Allen Hamilton. D.A.H. No cool nickname. Just a few initials that when strung together sound like a terrified kid stammering to answer some difficult math equation in front of his peers. So Jillian Stevens did contribute at least one thing to my life. She saved my name. Also, since Kara is over at Mom's house right now, at least she isn't here in the hospital bugging me. I guess that is two contributions.

Dad is sitting in the chair next to me, supposedly grading papers. He is an elementary school teacher, and he loves his job. Actually, he seems to be watching TV more than grading papers. Tonight is the opening of the Major League Baseball season, and we have the game on ESPN. So he is grading papers, and I am running, just like this morning. Except this time, I am running to the bathroom, hoping my episodes end soon.

Chapter 2

dash – (v): to depress or dispirit

For the first time in several months, the alarm sounded before my eyes were opened. Although it wasn't really my alarm, I will still concede defeat in the first race of the day. The buzzing sound actually came from some hospital contraption they hooked me up to last night. Despite my greatest fears, I got poked with a needle. They connected me to some IV tube, to replenish the liquids I had lost with all of my episodes yesterday. If I wasn't already thin as a rail, yesterday surely made me look like a teenage version of Flat Stanley. Maybe Dad could slip me into an envelope and mail me to each of the ballparks around Major League Baseball. That would be so tight!

     Dad and I share several common interests. We both love running. For as long as I can remember, he used to take me with him on his weekend runs through the local forest preserves. We'd wake up early on a Saturday or Sunday morning, throw on our running gear, and drive over to the preserve. After a few minutes of stretching, we were off. Though he could run like a deer, Dad always modified his pace so I could keep up. We ran, stride for stride, side by side. It's similar to how we have done most everything. He has always been there for me. Even during the worst year of my life. Dad is constant.

Unlike other runners who are totally hooked up to their iPods or cell phones, Dad and I run device-free. If we are not shooting the breeze about school, baseball, girls, or the latest book, we just run silently and soak up the sounds of nature that surround us. No distractions. No interference. Just me, Dad, and freedom.

Besides running, Dad is all about learning. He says that life is the greatest classroom. He loves learning, and he loves being around kids who have that same passion and curiosity. I think that's what makes him such a great teacher – he has such a child-like awe of the world around him. I swear, he asks more questions about things than I do. We'll be running through the woods, and Dad will notice a few deer sitting pensively in the brush, and he will ask me "Why are those deer crouched down? What are they gazing at"? One time we were on a crowded train zipping downtown, and there were a few kids on board who were totally out of control. They were shouting while tossing various toys to each other from across the aisle, and their mom didn't seem to notice at all. Two older women, sitting in front of the distracted mom and her unruly clan, were obviously unnerved by the whole scene. Dad leaned over to me and whispered "Why do you think that mom is oblivious to her kids?" I had no idea, but I could tell that the two older women were fed up and about to intervene. Sensing their impatience, Dad made his way over to the mother of three. "Are you alright? Is there anything I can do for you"?

Emerging from her fog, the bleary-eyed woman responded that she and her boys were returning from a memorial service for their father, who had just been killed while serving in the military overseas. She tried to apologize for any commotion her children had caused, but my dad just pulled up a seat and allowed her to grieve. I followed his lead, and sat down with her three boys, and we had a great time talking about their favorite baseball players. The two older women slunk down in their seats, probably ashamed of their own irritation.

Once or twice a week it seems Dad and I find ourselves in a bookstore or library, perusing all sorts of treasures. He loves many genres, but is especially fond of non-fiction reading. One day, he will be knee-deep in architecture books, and the next visit, I'll find him digging through books on Ancient China, or scanning the pages of the latest guide on Texas Hold 'Em. I'm usually in the biography section, reading various perspectives on some of my idols such as Martin Luther King Jr., Steve Prefontaine, or Teddy Roosevelt. Of course, most of my visits also include time looking through the latest running and / or baseball magazines.

Reading is Dad's form of tackling. He tackles his questions and wonders by reading as much as he can. When he encounters a new idea, or when doesn't understand something, he gathers piles of books and articles on the subject, and dives right in. He is relentless. Like a kid in a candy store, he wanders enthusiastically through aisles of books, grabbing all sorts of new insights and understanding. It is inspiring to watch him when he is on his frequent quests.

He tackles life's most difficult obstacles in the same way. When Mom left him to "find herself" several years ago, our dining room turned into a revolving library. There were stacks of books, ranging from topics like "How to be a Successful Single Parent", to "Dads Raising Strong-Willed Daughters", and "Making Sure your Young Man Measures Up". Dad was resolved that our family was going to make it through that ordeal. While it has been a rocky road, he has carried us through so far.

Later that same year, after Grandpa Stevens passed, Dad began reading books dealing with grief, and honoring the memories and traditions of lost loved ones. I don't think I would have made it through if dad hadn't helped me talk about Grandpa's passing. I was totally heartbroken.

I really crashed about a week after the funeral. I think I cried as much that night, as I puked last night. I just couldn't stop. I had been pretty quiet for several days, and had even stopped running. Dad tried to get me to talk, but I didn't know how. Then one day, during track practice after school, Forrest made some wise crack to me about why I didn't want to run that day, and told me to suck it up. That was all it took. I laid into him with all the fury my wiry frame could muster, and had that mammoth jerk pinned to the ground in record time. Coach Fitz had to pull me off, and then suspended me from the team. I told him it wasn't necessary, that I had quit. Then I sunk to a new low when I tossed out the crack that the team had no chance the rest of the season without me. I was such a jerk.

That night, Dad sat me down on the backyard trampoline, and we just looked up at the stars and sat quietly. He didn't push, he just waited. We both did. I figured sooner or later he would scold me, but he just sat quietly and let me work things through inside. Finally, he took my hand, and the tears started.

"I really miss Grandpa."

"Me too, son."

"It hurts so much, Dad."

"I know. Grandpa really loved you. He was so proud of you."

"You think so?"

"Of course."

"But I didn't visit him after he left. After she left."

"He understood, son."

"Are you sure?"

"Yes. I'm positive. Grandpa was a wise and patient man. He always understood."

Eventually, we made our way indoors. Dad grabbed a few blankets, and threw a log on the fire. I cuddled near the fireplace, and he brought down "The Collection". And "The Shoes".

Grandpa Stevens had started a collection of autographed baseballs for me. When I was just a few years old, he took me to see the Yankees when they came to town to play our White Sox. Now we hated the Yankees as much as anybody, but Grandpa loved certain players, regardless of what teams they happened to play for. He wanted me to see Derek Jeter. "This young man is special, Dash. He plays the game the right way. Take notice." I was in awe that

Grandpa could cheer for players on opposing teams. He was always more of a character guy than a stat guy.

That night, he secured a Derek Jeter autograph for me, the first ball in my collection. Since then, I have been given signed balls from Cal Ripken, Joe Mauer, Ron Santo, and my personal favorite, Robin Ventura. Like Grandpa, character guys. Grandpa eventually gave me balls from his own collection. I have one from Triple-Crown winner Carl Yaztremski, and balls from Rod Carew, Joe Morgan, and Roberto Clemente. Grandpa used to tell me that Clemente was the best player he ever saw play the game.

In front of the warming fire, Dad and I looked over the balls. Character guys. I felt ashamed. Guys like Carew, Clemente and Ventura weren't quitters. These guys were determined men who left it all out on the field. They overcame obstacles on soldiered on. They put in the hard work day after day, year after year. They put their teams first above personal accolades.

Then I looked at the shoes. The first pair of Nikes I ever owned. When I first showed a passion for running, Grandpa took me to a real running store to get a pair of customized racing shoes. He had the staff perform specialized tests while I ran on a treadmill, examining my gait and stride, and determining whether I was a heel, mid-foot, or fore-foot striker when I ran. Then he let me pick out a pair of shoes. They were Aqua-marine with a lime-green swoosh, matching laces, and fluorescent-yellow soles. They felt like silk slippers on my feet. Grandpa even inscribed the sentiment from his favorite quote on them as a message for me. It is from Helen Keller who said "*Life is either a daring adventure or nothing at all.*" On the toe box of my left shoe he wrote "DARING", and the toe box on my right he penned "ADVENTURE". I remember tripping the first few times I ran in them, trying to look at those two words with each stride, hoping to sear them into my brain as a lifelong mantra. I wanted to be daring. Like him. I wanted to experience adventure. When I finally outgrew that first pair, Grandpa had them bronzed for my birthday. I can still see his message.

"Dad, I need to call Coach Fitz."

"It's after 10pm son. Talk to him tomorrow."

"Dad, please? I need to set things right, immediately."

"Sure son."

"And, um, do you think Forrest is still awake"?

I needed a little extra sauce on the crow I had to swallow that night. Forrest made sure to rub it in every chance he had over the next few weeks, but at least Coach let me back on the team. After I apologized to the whole squad. It was hard, but it was the right thing to do.

Grandpa Stevens used to live with us. Grandma had died when I was too little to remember, and Mom and Dad asked Grandpa to move in and help raise his grandson. I'm glad he accepted. When Mom and Dad would leave for work, we used to play catch out back. While Dad taught me how to pitch a baseball, it was Grandpa who taught me how to play defense and run the bases. When there was a game on the TV, he would sit me on his lap, and show me what clues to look for in a pitcher's delivery, as well as how to notice the positioning of the infielders. He would record the games with great base-stealers, and have me watch their techniques over and over. He taught me how a base stealer's greatest weapon wasn't his speed, but his instincts. Every time I reach first base in a game, Grandpa's words still echo in my head, reminding me about the importance of my technique. Thanks to his tutelage, I have led our league in steals three years running.

On the nights that Dad was unable to read to me, Grandpa would come into my room, pull the chair beside my bed, and read various baseball biographies to me. From Babe Ruth to Brooks Robinson, Grandpa would share stories of some of his all-time favorite players. At the morning breakfast table, he would pour over box scores with me, showing me who got clutch hits, or made key sacrifices for their team to win the night before. And of course, we always checked who swiped bases in last night's contests.

After she moved out, everything changed.

It wasn't long before Grandpa started in on his lectures. Instead of reading me biographies on Gehrig, Aaron, Mays or Koufax, I was getting almost nightly messages about my "attitude problem". He told me I needed to forgive her. He promised me that she still loved all of us, but that something was "broken" inside of her. He promised she would come back eventually.

I wasn't buying it.

How could a loving mother leave her wonderful husband, two young kids, and an ailing father? How was that loving?

She said she needed to find herself. It seems to me that she lost herself by leaving us. I know she lost me.

Within a few months, Grandpa decided it was his fault that she left. He said that he felt like he was in the way, and that we would be better off as a family if he gave us some space. It was hard enough that mom ran out on us, but now Grandpa was going as well? He moved across town into a facility that is part hospital, part senior home.

After he left, I couldn't bring myself to visit him. I'm not sure why. I hated hospitals. I couldn't stand seeing all those slow, weak, feeble people. I'd always been afraid of needles, even though there is one embedded in my arm right now. Maybe I was angry about those lectures. I wasn't ready to forgive Mom, and I didn't want my visits to Grandpa to be more long discussions about opening my heart to a mother who closed her own heart to me. So I never visited him. I wanted to. I planned to. I just hadn't gotten there yet.

Then he left for real. Passed away before I got to say goodbye.

Chapter 3

dash – (n): a violent and rapid blow or stroke

Whatever this bug is, it really has me off my game. Besides sleeping later than normal, I have no appetite whatsoever. Of course my stomach hurts, after spending yesterday stuck on the spin cycle. Dad looks pretty rough too. He stayed in the chair next to my bed, and his clothes are pretty disheveled after a restless night. I wonder if he slept at all.

We turned on ESPN this morning to catch the late night scores, and then the doctor stopped by and asked dad "if she could have a moment". They stepped out into the hall a while ago, but I haven't heard any talking. I guess after their conversation, Dad must have needed to stretch his legs, and maybe run down to the cafeteria to grab a morning coffee and the paper.

I really feel bad about Dad having to be here with me. He has had so much to deal with after she left. I try real hard to be a good son, but I know I must be a lot to deal with. First of all, Kara and I seem to fight all the time. That girl just has a knack for getting under my skin. If she isn't constantly sneaking in my room going through my stuff, then she is in her "diva" mode, singing and prancing around the house. It is ironic. Mom named me after a musician, and I couldn't be less interested in music. Dad named Kara after one of the world's best female runners, Kara Goucher, and our Kara doesn't give a hoot about running. Maybe if she did, we would get along better. But no; she is a singer through and through. She sings in the shower. Sure, I guess many people sing in their shower, but she's so loud, and if you ask me, (though I'm no "American Idol" judge), she is rather "pitchy". She sings in the car. Again, extremely loud. It seems like she wants the whole world to stop and listen. She sings in her room at night as she is getting ready to sleep (though it makes sleeping really difficult for the rest of us). She sings at the breakfast table. I mean really, wouldn't that annoy anyone? How can I concentrate on reading the box scores? Dad tells me it is just how she is "wired", and that I need to learn to enjoy her. That's easy for him to say though, since she is *his* daughter. I had no choice in the matter.

What really bugs me is that she seems totally cool with what mom did to us. Kara loves visiting mom every other weekend, and talks to her on the phone almost daily. They go to movies, plays, and musicals whenever they can, and Kara goes out of her way to find out what outfits mom is going to wear to a show, so she can dress like her. Ugh. How a daughter can accept a mom who ran out on her is beyond me. At least, her relationship with mom keeps her out of my hair a lot. I guess I can enjoy that about her.

On top of trying to keep peace between me and Kara, Squirt is no picnic to deal with either. After Grandpa Stevens left, Dad thought it would be a good idea if we got a dog. At the animal shelter, Kara and I both fell in love with this tiny little sandy-colored Shih-Tzu that had come out of the wrong end of a scuffle with an overly aggressive Rottweiler. His right eye closed frequently, the result of some nerve damage from the attack. Kara and I just figured that the little pup was winking at us. It was love at first sight. In a rare warm moment between the two of us, we mutually agreed to name him Squirt, since he was so frail and tiny.

True to his name, Squirt has remained tiny and adorable. He couldn't have been happier to wind up in a safe, loving home. Also, true to his name, he "squirts". I'm sure he doesn't mean to make such a mess. It's just that whenever the little guy gets nervous or excited, he tends to pee a bit. He is an easily excitable, and therefore highly messy, dog. Whenever someone approaches our door, he squirts. When he sees other dogs, whether outside our window or on the television, he squirts. If you try to play a game with him, like having him fetch a toy or wrestle with an old sock, he squirts. Even sometimes when Kara really belts her songs, he squirts, (which might actually be a fitting tribute to some of her singing). After a few days of cleaning up one stain after another, Dad pleaded with Kara and I to consider returning Squirt for a different dog. He even resorted to bribery, offering to buy season's passes to the Six Flags Theme Park if we would just give up

Squirt. Thankfully, Kara was as totally sold on Squirt as I was, and Dad relented. He decided to remove all the carpeting in the house and install wood flooring. He spent his entire summer break on his hands and knees, installing those floors in every room in our home. His knees and back ached for weeks, but at least we could easily clean up after Squirt with a quick wipe of a paper towel. What a dad.

Since she left, he has never gone out on a date. I can tell by the way that some of the ladies look at him when we are out in the stores that he wouldn't have any problem meeting someone, but like Grandpa, he still believes in miracles. Why is it that I'm the only one in this family who has been able to accept reality and move on?

After the TV analysts finished their breakdown of last night's opening game, Dad finally came back into the room. There was no coffee, just a blank expression on his face. I recognized that glazed looked in his eyes. It was the same expression he had when he told us that mom left. It was the same look when he had to break the news about Grandpa's passing. No words were necessary. I could see it in his eyes. Whatever the doctor had said to him was bad. Real bad.

"Son, this bug you have, isn't the flu."

The clocks in our room must have seized up, because that moment seemed frozen. My skin tingled.

Whatever energy I had that day seemed to drain from me, while I waited for Dad to finish his sentence.

"Son..."

"Dash..."

"The doctor says you have cancer."

Cancer. Is there a more dreaded word in anyone's vocabulary?

Looking back on that moment, I'm sure that I must have been scared, or perhaps just in denial, but something weird began to take place. It was as if Dad and I did a role-reversal. I dove into a protective mode, trying to shelter my dad from encountering even more pain in his life. He had been through so much already, and there was no way that I was going to add to his troubles. Sitting up in my bed, I opened my arms to him, and he fell right in.

For several minutes, we sat just there; father and son, engulfing the room with a delicate silence, as I held him close.

"Don't worry. It's gonna be okay."

"We'll get through this."

"Sigh. You have always been so strong."

"You know we're gonna beat this thing."

"Yeah. We'll be together every step of the way."

"I love you, Dad."

Chapter 4

dashing – (adj): energetic and spirited; lively.

"Morbid appearances". Supposedly, this is what the doctor found when reviewing the tests that had been performed on me. She says one of the blood tests revealed that my lymph nodes have developed the cancer known as Hodgkin's lymphoma. A quick web search will tell you that the illness was named after Thomas Hodgkin, who in 1832 discovered a pattern of disease in the lymph nodes of preserved human specimens. *Preserved human specimens?* Yuck! I don't even want to know.

Hodgkin wrote a paper, entitled "*On Some Morbid Appearances of the Absorbent Glands and Spleen.*" Given his "morbid" description, I'm not sure that I ever want to see my lymph nodes under any microscope. It wasn't bad enough that blood and needles made me queasy; now I have some "morbid" thing developing inside of me. Definitely not something to score any "cool" points with the girls. I really have my work cut out for me.

After Dad and I let the news settle in regarding my diagnosis, he got busy. Doctor Lunzer, the cancer specialist, provided him with various pamphlets regarding treatment possibilities, and then Dad jumped on his laptop and started searching for articles and books about this disease. He looks like he should have shoulder pads and a helmet on – he's in full tackling mode.

Before he grabbed the laptop, I found out a few interesting facts about my disease. Apparently Hodgkin's lymphoma forms in the very regions of your body that are meant to fight disease and illness. We each have an immune system, set up to protect our bodies from various sicknesses and infections, and a significant part of this defense system is comprised of a network of vessels and nodes that transport our white blood cells. This system is known as the lymph system, and is found in virtually every part of our body, although some of the largest clusters of the lymph nodes are found in the underarms, groin, neck and abdomen.

Symptoms associated with my disease include fever (doesn't every sickness?), night sweats, unexplained weight loss, and itchy skin. The list hardly seems helpful in identifying cancer in this teenager. I had assumed any "night sweats" were just my body attempting to cool down from the frequent late night sprints I run to take advantage of the cool evening air. Unexplained weight loss? I have never experienced any significant weight gain to begin with, and have been chronically slender. Most track teams are populated by beanpoles like me. And as for itchy skin, I have always associated my dry skin with the changing seasons here in the Midwest. When fall gives way to winter, my skin usually requires constant applications of lotion, or I will be scratching the skin off my legs, stomach and arms. The same goes for when winter blossoms into spring – out comes the lotion bottle. Joey usually just tells me that my skin looks "ashy".

How could I have seen this coming?

We are waiting for Dr. Lunzer to return so we can discuss the treatment options with her. With the county track meets just a couple weeks away, I don't want to lose any ground in my training. The last thing I want is to supply Forrest with something else to gloat about, and if I don't beat him in this race, I will never hear the end of it. Plus, it wouldn't hurt to score a few points with Kelly by giving Forrest the beat-down he so richly deserves. Perhaps then she would start noticing me a bit more, and forget about that little incident on the Durham's front lawn. Fortunately, today was scheduled to be a cross-training day working on my upper-body strength, and tomorrow is slated as my one day of rest each week, so this won't set me back too much. I just hate being cooped up in here.

Talk about stir crazy – I cannot wait to bounce from this place. Besides the groans and coughs I hear wafting in from the corridor, this room is so dreary. Everything is a shade of gray. Gray walls. Gray ceiling tiles. Even the plastic covers on the light fixtures have a dull yellow-gray fade burned into them. The curtains dividing the room look they used to be light blue, but have grayed with age. The floor tiles are worn-dirty-white, and bespeckled with gray flecks, presumably to add interest. I'm going crazy imprisoned in this monochromatic infirmary.

Not counting the TV remote that is joined to my bedpost by a cord, I have counted seven different contraptions that are either connected to me, or that are plugged into other machines. A few of them have alarms, or beeps that must tell the hospital staff something about my condition. Every thirty minutes or so some nurse walks in, adjusts a knob or tube, winks at me, and makes a note on my chart. When they ask me how I am feeling, I try to begin a little playful chatter with them about how I'd rather be out for a run or at the ballpark. They simply nod, give an awkward smile and exit to continue their rounds.

I wonder what all these machines are for. Assuming one of them keeps track of my vital signs, and maybe another one tracks how I respond to medications, I am still at a loss for what functions the other gadgets perform. It would be a little reassuring if the doctor explained them to me. Better yet, just disconnect me and let me out of here already.

"Dad, when is Dr. Lunzer returning?"

"I'm not sure son. I thought she'd be back by now. Let me finish this article and go ask the nurse. Do you need me to get you anything?"

After asking my dad to grab some chips or crackers for a snack, he left my dingy coop to track down the whereabouts of our doctor. A few restless minutes later, I grabbed my phone and texted Joey. Apparently word gets around. Joey replied that he already knew I was in the hospital, but wasn't sure what landed me here. I wasn't prepared to get into the specifics yet, especially via text, but I really wanted some live company. I texted back:

"Got really sick yday. Puking evrywhere. Dr. runnin tests. Can u visit?"

After a couple minutes, Joey texted that he would have his mom drop him off in an hour or so. He also let me know that he was going to smuggle in a pocketful of candy to "refresh my taste buds". That's my best friend for you.

I have a hard time recalling a time when Joey didn't have a pocketful of candy. It seems as if he has always had a pipeline to the local confectionary in there. It didn't matter what the occasion was, Joey would always pull some type of sweet treat out of his pocket. During baseball season, when other kids try to look cool spitting sunflower seeds, Joey is a happy camper sucking on a stash of lemonheads. At lunch, he always has an assortment of starburst or skittles that he pulls out, offering to share. I'm not sure how clean those pockets are, but when it comes to candy, I usually abide by Joey's mantra – "Eat now, Question later."

Of course, that philosophy nearly cost Joey dearly when he was a little kid. As the story goes, he was out back swimming with his siblings in the family pool, when his mom came out and tossed a couple of white tablets into the water. Assuming she was playing some kind of game with her kids by tossing candy into the pool, Joey went into "fetch" mode, and dove underneath the water to retrieve the sweets. He came up gloating how he had "won" by getting the candies first, and gulped his treasure down before someone could stop him. His older brother Steve began scolding him; "Those weren't candies, you idiot! Those were chlorine tablets to clean the pool water!" His mother yanked Joey from the pool, and he wound up getting his stomach flushed with milk for a considerable portion of the afternoon, until the doctors were sure that there was no danger from the chlorine he swallowed. He detests milk to this day, but still dives in headfirst when it comes to candy.

Dad finally returns, and he is visibly upset.

"What's up, Dad?"

"Dash, it seems there has been a misunderstanding. I was under the impression that Dr. Lunzer was going to return later this morning so she could discuss the treatment options with us. It seems as if there are a few more tests she wants to run before the hospital is going to release us. Then we will return later in the week to review the options on how to move forward."

"Nooo! Can't we just get out of here now, Dad? We can come back later for the tests."

"I wish we could, son. I know this is really hard."

"How much longer is it going to be?"

"They aren't sure, but they think we will be done with the tests later tonight. Your mom called, and she is going to bring Kara by to visit you. Your mom would really like to visit you as well."

"But I already texted Joey! He should be coming by in a little while. Can't I just visit with him? I'll see Kara when we get home, anyway."

"Your sister, and your mom, are both concerned Dash. It would really be good if you would let them visit for a while."

"Daaad, I really don't want to deal with this right now! Not here. Not today."

"I'll tell you what. I'll call them and let them know that Joey is stopping by. I'll have them wait a bit and then come by later this afternoon."

"Ugh. Fine."

Great. Not only do I have more tests (which undoubtedly means more poking and prodding will be involved), but now I have to deal with her. My cage is shrinking.

Chapter 5

dash – (v): to confound or abash

After trouncing me in eight consecutive Mario Kart races on our DS' game systems, Joey sensed that I was out of sorts. Normally, I'm as competitive as they come, and have been known to let a few expletives fly if I lose some type of contest. Today, Joey said I had become downright angelic; a complete rollover in our matches.

"What's up, Dash? Why such a wuss in the games today?"

"Hey! Cut me some slack! With all these gizmos hooked up to me, I didn't exactly catch a good night's rest last night. I'm just a bit out of it today."

"Whatevs. So do the doctors know what made you sick?"

"Well, sort of. They think that they found a little bit of something called Hodgkin's disease in my lymph nodes."

"Uh, I'm not sure what that means. Are you contagious? Are you gonna get any skinnier? If you lose any more weight, it'll be impossible for Kelly to notice you. Do you have to take some nasty medicines? "

For whatever reason, I just didn't want to get into it with Joey. I wasn't ready to explain the "C-word". Truthfully, I was tired, but I think I was more anxious than anything else. Besides worrying about the training I was missing, I knew that Mom and Kara would be here any minute. I had been working hard to avoid interactions with Mom, and today she had me cornered. I explained to Joey that I should be out of here later tonight, and I'd text him once I got home.

As Joey left, I saw Dad fiddling with his phone, and figured that Mom and Kara must have texted him that they were here. Sure enough, Dad snuck out for a few minutes, probably to give them the low down on my status before they came into the room. Now my heart was racing.

There was a time when I used to love hanging out with Mom. A couple years before she felt like she needed to go off and "find herself", I remember that she used to be quite the affectionate one. She had this way of making you feel like you were living inside of a musical. In the mornings, instead of an alarm waking us up, Mom would come into our rooms, comb her fingers through our hair, and invite us into a new day with the enchanting melody of her voice. Whether it was show tunes from her youth, or pop music from the radio, Mom would weave magic with her singing.

If either Kara or I were having a bad day, Mom would wrap us in her arms, and just listen as we poured out whatever was bothering us. I remember once when I was out in the back, on a pitching mound I had formed in our yard, practicing the "Nolan Ryan" fastball that Dad had taught me. It slipped through my hand, shattering the second-floor window. Dad was livid with me, but Mom could see I was genuinely upset with myself for the wild pitch, and after letting me lean into her blouse and cry my eyes out, she calmed me (and Dad) down with her own whimsical rendition of "Take Me Out to the Ballgame".

"Take me out to the backyard
Take me to Dash's mound
Buy me some peanuts and brand new glass
I don't care that the old window cracked.
Oh it's root, root, root
For my all-star
Whose speed will bring him to fame
For its one, two, three strikes - you're out!
At the old ball game!"

I still have no idea what happened, but after a while, her music just dried up. Mom grew to be consistently cranky, her singing replaced by sniping, and her calming choruses replaced by constant complaining. The vibrant, happy mother slowly vanished. Then, she left altogether, shattering our family. We have been painstakingly picking up the shards these past several years, but for me, the cracks remain.

After spending a couple years in New York pursuing her musical interests, Mom moved back to the area. She got a small place on the other side of town, supposedly so she could be back by me and Kara. I made it clear from the beginning that I had no intention of throwing her a welcoming party, but both Dad and Kara seem pretty cool with her being back. Besides Kara's visits every other weekend, Dad will go by occasionally and fix a leaky pipe or paint a room. I think they have even had a couple dinners together. Kara and I can tell that he never stopped loving her, and that he hopes she'll want to move back in someday. I certainly hope not. She made her choice. Let her live with it.

It's odd having her back in town. When I go for my long runs, I make sure to stay on our side of the town. Sometimes though, I have the odd sensation that she is lurking around the corner. Every once in a while, I catch a glimpse of a woman with her hair scrunched beneath a baseball cap and her face hidden behind a huge pair of sunglasses, and I think it is her. At one of our games last month, I cracked a walk-off double, and heard a woman yelp "Way to go, Dash!" I could have sworn it was her voice. I scanned the stands looking for her, but the woman with the hat and sunglasses just fixed her stare at the ground.

When the phone rings, I look at the caller ID before picking up, just to avoid talking to her. A few times, when coming over to pick up Kara, she comes inside to visit, and asks me to come along, but I just shrug and let her know that I am too busy with baseball or track. She has even resorted to sending me a few letters. I'm not proud to admit it, but let's just say that I let Squirt do his thing with them.

Grandpa wouldn't be happy with me. In his lectures, he tried to get me to believe that someday Mom would come back. He kept telling me that even though she made a terrible choice by walking out on us, that Mom, Dad, Kara and I would always be "family", even if we didn't live together. He believed that perhaps Mom's choices would lead to some sort of miraculous journey, resulting in a family that once again loved being with each other.

How could that be? She proved that she loved being on her own with her music more than her family. She proved that she was willing to leave us to pursue "her dreams". Why didn't Kara, and moreover Dad, see that?

"Hi Dash. How ya doing?"

Kara and Mom entered the room.

"Hi son. Kara and I wanted to stop by and see how you're doing."

"Hi Kara. Hi Mom. Um, thanks for coming."

Kara came right up and sat on the edge of the bed, while Mom chose to sit in the chair over by the window. Things were getting really awkward, really fast.

"Dad tells us that you need a few more tests, and then you'll be home tonight. I'm really sorry that you're sick, Dash. Is there anything I can do for you?"

"No, but thanks. How is Squirt?"

"Aw, he's fine. I think he wondered where you were last night. He kept looking in your room for you. After a while, he decided it was the best place to wait for you. So he hopped up and made himself at home on your pillow."

"Oh no. Did he, you know, 'squirt' on it?"

"Ewww! For your sake I hope not! But I didn't think to check this morning."

"Great."

"We saw Joey on the way out. He said you were feeling a bit 'wussy' today. What's that all about?"

"Just Joey being Joey."

After some more small talk, Kara wandered off into the hall, probably looking for Dad. There went my security blanket.

With a few more minutes of surreal silence, Mom eventually scooted her chair over to my bedside. Tentatively, she placed her hand on the bed, and started talking.

"How's the training been going?"

"Pretty good, thanks."

"I hear you're preparing for a big upcoming meet. What events are you running in?"

"Um, the usual. I have a few short events, and the mile run."

"What kind of times are you doing for the mile lately?"

"Um, I don't know. Around five minutes."

"Oh. That sounds good..."

There. I hope she got the hint. Between making no eye contact with her, replying in stilted, hushed phrases, and pretending I wasn't keenly aware of my running times, I think she heard the screams coming from deep inside of me that I wanted to be anywhere else but here. I couldn't handle being trapped in this gray prison, with her gray presence bringing me down.

A few more minutes of silence hung in the room before a nurse came in (God bless that woman!) instructing Mom that I was going to be taken for some kind of scan. As I was wheeled away, I fervently hoped that this test would outlast Mom's desire to stay in the room.

The nurse took me to the basement, through a hallway lined with all types of pipes and wires. We emerged into a lab of sorts, and the staff there helped me up onto a flat metal table which fed into a long narrow tube. Since the paper-thin robe I was wearing only covered my front side, my bare back flinched against the cold steel table. I tried my best to lift my back in an attempt to levitate above the frigid slate, but my strength failed me and an infantry of goose bumps marched up my arms. The nurse retreated behind a plexi-glass barrier, no doubt keeping comfortably warm, and called out a litany of instructions for the scan, reminding me to remain perfectly still and silent during what she promised would be a short test. As the table crept forward into the tube, I closed my eyes, feeling like a hot dog encased in a very small porcelain bun.

After a few minutes inside, I began to wonder if the nurse had forgotten that I was still in the chamber. Did she leave for a snack break? Other than the whir of a distant fan, there was a creepy silence in the remote basement lab. I wanted to call out, but I had been told to remain silent. My nose began to itch. I accidentally had what Dad commonly refers to as a "one-cheek-sneak", when a not-too silent fart escaped. *Yikes! Did anyone hear that? Will that show up on the scan somehow? Ewwww – that was a bad one!* A really foul odor took custody of the chamber.

As if on cue, the nurse finally came and removed me from the tube (and the "fog" I left in there). I'm not positive, but it seemed as if she scrunched up her nose when she was helping me back into my wheelchair.

Exhausted and embarrassed, I was grateful that she brought me back up to my room. As we crossed into doorway, Mom was still at my bedside. Darn. She explained to me that Dad had taken Kara out for a quick bite and that he would be back in a while to bring me home, as soon as the hospital was ready to release me. Once the nurse left, I was once again all alone with Mom, for only the second time since she walked out on us, both times today.

"Dexter, I just wanted to...."

"It's Dash, Mom."

"Right. Sorry. Dash, I just wanted to see if we could clear the air between us. I realize you're still upset about what I did..."

"Mom, I really don't want to talk about it. It's in the past."

"You're right. It's in the past. So how do we go on from here?"

"Mom, I'm really tired. Can we please not get into this?"

Sigh.

"Sure. I just want you to know, as I have said in my letters, I'm terribly sorry. I wish I could go back and change everything, but I know I can't. Leaving this family was the worst decision I ever made in my life. Leaving Dad, you and Kara was foolish and selfish. I know I hurt you all, and I only hope someday, somehow, that I can make things right."

Her words drifting in the air, my chest tightened and my eyes stung, as I rolled over to face the window straining to get away from this moment, this heartache. Memories knocked at the door, and I pushed hard to keep them from entering. Similar to cooling down after a long run, I concentrated on my breathing, trying to center my racing thoughts. Long, deep breaths. Drawing in. Holding. Releasing. Calming. Searching for peace.

"Dash. I'm truly sorry. I hope someday you can forgive me."

Deep breaths. Drawing in. Holding. Releasing.

"I love you, son."

My back pressed against memories, against her, desperately trying to prevent myself from cracking inside. I was so tired, and so drained. I yearned for sleep, for comfort, and for escape. After lying silent for as long as I could, I heard the nurse come in. She propped me up in my bed, and began to disconnect some of the machinery I had been hooked up to. Mom was gone. Just as I thought. How typical of her. She's good at leaving.

Glancing at the side table, I notice she left behind a photo and a book. The picture is very familiar. I am much younger, sitting on Grandpa Stevens lap, no doubt soothed by the scent of his Old Spice cologne, clasping the new baseball mitt Mom had given me as a birthday present. She is on our left, while Kara is leaning against Grandpa's right side. Dad was behind the camera. We were all together, smiling. Then she tore us apart.

Overcome by emotion, I ripped the right side of the photo, leaving only the image of Grandpa, myself, and Kara intact. Lifting the book, I notice the title: "*The Miraculous Journey of Edward Tulane*", and recall Grandpa's wishes that Mom could have some type of miraculous journey of her own. There was no way that I was going read that book, so I tossed the image of Mom inside the cover, and threw a sidearm delivery of the book into the hallway. It landed with a pleasant thud.

Chapter 6

dash – (v): to ruin or frustrate hopes or plans, etc.

With reluctance, I wave at a lady with a dusting of silver hair as she jogs by, realizing that she must be the dozenth runner I've crossed paths with in the forest preserve this morning. Training later than normal, I notice the running trails seem more like the main roads at rush hour, congested with bikers, dog walkers, moms with strollers, and runners of all ages coming and going. Maintaining a steady pace is virtually impossible, and witnessing aging adults run with relative ease compared to me, is downright discouraging.

Landmarks that I use as markers, like the crippled willow, or the recently installed curved cedar bridge, take longer to reach than I am accustomed to. Before I have even reached my second mile, there is a burning in my rib cage that usually only comes when I am executing my "kick" at the end of the run.

Though I should be concentrating on my breathing, all I can think about is how I would empty my savings account for an ice cold Gatorade right now.

Like the forest preserve, it seems as if all my paths have grown busy and complicated these past few weeks.

First off, my training schedule has been thrown out of whack because of the treatments I'm receiving. To cure the Hodgkin's lymphoma, I've started chemotherapy, going every three weeks. There are a total of six treatments. This past Monday marked two down, and four to go. Originally, Dr. Lunzer had scheduled the treatments for Fridays, in order that I miss as little school as possible. Patients tend to feel pretty rough the first 24-48 hours after chemo, and the thinking was that I could use weekends to recover. But since the county meet was scheduled for this coming Saturday, I knew there was no way I could compete, much less hit my best mile time, just one day out of chemo. I fought to have my treatments scheduled earlier in the week. Knowing how important my training is to me, Dad and Dr. Lunzer eventually consented, and my chemo was moved to Mondays. Still, I have been losing serious ground on my goals, and my mile time has slipped with almost every practice. The county meet is now only three days away, and I'm worried.

The treatments are brutal. When I get to the hospital, they whisk me into my own "chemo suite", complete with TV and DVD player. I am allowed to have a friend join me in the room while I'm getting the chemo, but so far I've just asked Dad to hang with me. After they get me all hooked up, it takes nearly five hours to pump the medications into me. Sitting in that little box of a room, the arms of the clock weighed down, it feels more like ten. At least I have Dad.

Around the second day after the chemo, I usually feel like a tackling dummy, with my body aching from head to toe. Today is that second day. My head feels like a scuffed up bowling ball, and though my arms look fine, they feel like they should be blue and purple, covered with bruises. What train hit me? Despite the anti-nausea meds, my gut had been wrenching all morning, so I decided to run a couple hours later in the hopes that my strength would improve. My stomach still feels as if it's gingerly toting a case of champagne glasses that I must keep from breaking with each stride, and I am easily parched even though I'm running way behind my normal pace. Finally I set my bravado aside, and pull up before crossing the cedar bridge, deciding to cut my training short this morning. I'll try to finish later tonight.

Another complication from the past few weeks is the new diet Dad has me on. Unlike Joey with his affinity for sweets, I have considered myself a relatively healthy eater for someone my age. After my diagnosis though, Dad scoured several books and websites, searching for foods that would help me in this battle against cancer. I was hoping we would find various tasty fruits that would combat the cancer cells inside me, or perhaps some zesty recipe for steak. Outside of dark chocolate however, it seems that the only foods which possess the killer instinct for cancer, also have the characteristic of killing off all the pleasure in your taste buds!

For instance, Dad is loading me up on Japanese Green Tea. Blech! I never could stomach coffee or tea, but apparently green tea is listed as one of the most potent weapons to battle cancer. I guess since I've been able to handle some of the putrid tasting athletic drinks in my training, I should be able to stomach the bitter taste of the tea. He is also filling up the cupboard with pomegranate juice. The first week, we tried actually buying fresh pomegranates at the organic food store and juicing them ourselves, but it was a near impossible task with all of those hard seeds encrusted in the fruit. After a few minutes trying to extract the juice from the fruit, Dad's favorite dress shirt looked like he had been testing a pink tie-dye for art class. Since then, he has resorted to the bottled juice, and I drink a tall glass with each meal.

The worst drink of all is a disgusting concoction called "Kombucha". It wouldn't be so bad if I didn't actually know what it was made of, but I made the mistake of scanning the net to check out what Dad was asking me to gulp down, and I stumbled on the ingredients. Though some people think it comes from a mushroom (which would be bad enough), Kombucha is actually a *living* colony of bacteria and yeast that, along with a dose of sugar, is added to black or green tea. Then we have to set the mix aside to ferment for a few days. It tastes like a bitter salad dressing. To make each batch of tea, Dad has to take a starter sample from an existing culture and then grow a new colony in a fresh jar. How yummy.

For a snack, Dad coaxed me into eating "live" flaxseed crackers. After learning about the tea with living cultures of bacteria and yeast, I decided that perhaps I'd rather not know what was in these crackers. The first time I tried one, I literally spit it out in my hand. It was so nasty! Now I smother each one in a spoonful of peanut butter (sans jalapenos) in order to get it down safely.

I have to admit, Kara has been a really good sport with the diet. In a show of support for me, she has been eating and drinking all of the various tea and snacks that Dad has me on. She even went so far as cooking up a tofu casserole for our family dinner last night. Honestly, it was atrocious, but I really appreciate the effort. Whenever she wasn't looking, I scooped some in my hand and snuck it under the dinner table. Squirt didn't seem to mind it at all.

Besides the attempt at making dinner, Kara and Dad have been pretty creative in their efforts to help me. At last count, there are a mind-boggling thirteen different prescriptions I am taking, some of which are designed to overcome the side-effects of other medications. Before heading out to run this morning, I went to the medicine cabinet and stumbled on another one of their projects – an ingenious labeling system. In order to keep me from being overwhelmed by all of these medications, Kara and Dad began using various colors of duct tape, and a dose of their vivacious vocabulary, on my orange medicine bottles. They put a different color of duct tape on the cap of each bottle, describing the purpose of the medicine inside. The innovative labels include, on green duct tape: "sprint pain killer" (for semi-manageable pains), on red duct tape: "marathon pain killer" (for the intense teary-eyed pains), on blue duct tape: "tummy tamer" (for nausea) and on purple duct tape one that needs no further explanation - "potent poop-passers".

It was a hilarious and touching moment. I was doubled over and had tears from the laughter.

Startled, Dad and Kara rushed to the bathroom to see what was going on. Worried when they found me bent over and blubbering, we were eventually able to share a hearty family laugh for the first time in a long while. In fact, it was the only time I recall Kara hugging me since Grandpa's funeral.

The intimacy of the moment soon dissipated.

After dinner, I was getting ready to head back over to the forest preserve to finish my training, when Kara and I got into a little scuffle.

"Are you going running again, Dash?"

"Yeah, sis. The meet is this Saturday, and I can't let Forrest beat me."

"Who cares about a silly race? You're trying to beat cancer! Can't you just forget about that idiot Forrest, anyway?"

"Forget about him!? Forrest!? It's bad enough he is the most popular kid in my grade. And he leads the baseball team in home runs. And all the girls like him. But he has never beaten me in a race. Never! And there is no way I am going to let him take over the title as the fastest kid in the school!"

"Dash, it's just a stupid race. You'll be back to beating him again after your treatments are finished. Can't you just wait?"

A purposeful slam of the back door on the way out was my response to her ridiculous question.

Dangling my feet over the cedar bridge, I gaze at the sunset as people run by. I should be running, training for the meet, and I actually feel fine tonight, but the only part of me racing - is my mind.

Thoughts collide, and I have difficulty making sense of the chaos inside me. Kara thinks that my training is a waste of time. Forrest has been consistently gaining on me at practice. Kelly doesn't seem to know that I have any talents at all, unless you count the ability to hurl in living technicolor. Mom keeps pressuring me to talk to her. To top everything off, Dad has been sounding an awful lot like Grandpa lately, wanting me to deal with the "attitude problem" he thinks that I have with Mom.

"Stupid race?" How could she say that? My ability to outrun everyone else was all I had. I would never be considered the smartest kid in school, and despite my best efforts, I never would be very popular, but at least I have always been faster than everyone. Even Forrest.

Especially Forrest.

For years I had to put up with his taunts, always insisting on calling me Dexter, and purposely pronouncing it in that high-pitched, nasally tone that made my name sound like I belonged with those castoff jack-in-the-boxes on the island of misfit toys.

Maybe it was time to face reality. Perhaps I am a misfit after all. What would Kelly ever see in a guy like me?

Screw this. I'm tired of other people making me feel like crap.

With that epiphany, I'm on my feet and running. Racing across the bridge. Outrunning the voices of my naysayers. Distancing myself from their negativity. My legs, and my rage, carry me out of the preserve and onto the monotone streets, where I run into the descending darkness.

Chapter 7

dash – (v): to strike or smash violently, esp. to break to pieces.

Morning comes, and passes, and I am still lying around at home. Not only am I nauseous, but my head tingles and I'm wondering if I overdid it on my run last night, since my leg really hurts. I've tried icing it, elevating it, and stretching it, but the pain above my left knee is getting worse, and I've been noticeably limping. When dad tries to massage the area, it is all I can do to hold back the tears.

"Dash, this doesn't feel like normal swelling. It seems like you have a knot in your muscles."

He waits on me, alternating hot and cold treatments to the sore area, in an attempt to unlock the muscles and bring down the swelling. I'm supposed to be running hill intervals after school today to keep up my speed and strength, but just trying to jog this morning brought searing pain, so I decide to stay off my feet and hang out with Dad. We read some of the latest running magazines, and discuss our plans for the Big Sur Marathon next spring. Dad will be turning 40, and to commemorate the event, he and I are going to be running the picturesque race along the California coast. It will be the first ever marathon-event for each of us, with him running the complete 26.2 miles, and me running the half-marathon distance and then meeting him at the finish line. He pulls up the website on his laptop, and we watch videos detailing the course. At one point, as you run along the bay, there is a gentleman dressed in a tuxedo with a grand piano along the roadside, playing classical music for all the racers as they pass. Supposedly, you can hear the music for several miles through the cove. It looks amazing!

He doesn't know it yet, but Kara and I have already planned his birthday gift. We have each been saving a portion of our allowance for the past few months, with the intention that after the marathon, we are going to have his shoes bronzed. Knowing how much I treasure the pair Grandpa had bronzed for me, I hope Dad will feel the same about these. It also feels good to find some common ground to work with Kara on. Though not really interested in running, she has already been looking online to buy a customized running shirt for Dad's big race. She found a site that let her create a shirt using a photo of runners crossing the bridge over Monterey Bay as the backdrop.

She had his name his name emblazoned on the front above the photo. On the back of the shirt, she condensed one of Dad's favorite quotes by Theodore Roosevelt:

"It is not the critic who counts: not the man who points out how the strong man stumbles or where the doer of deeds could have done better. The credit belongs to the man who is actually in the arena, whose face is marred by dust and sweat and blood, who strives valiantly, who errs and comes up short again and again, because there is no effort without error or shortcoming, but who knows the great enthusiasms, the great devotions, who spends himself for a worthy cause; who, at the best, knows, in the end, the triumph of high achievement, and who, at the worst, if he fails, at least he fails while daring greatly, so that his place shall never be with

those cold and timid souls who knew neither victory nor defeat."

She chose a few key phrases – "Get in the Arena", "Strive Valiantly", and "Dare Greatly" inscribing these on the back of the shirt. Viewing the proof online, it really looks amazing. Dad is going to really love it. Between saving for that and the bronzing, she hasn't kept any of her allowance for weeks. I'll try to remember that next time I get so frustrated with her.

By mid afternoon, I can't even make it to the bathroom without crawling, and Dad decides to take me back to the hospital to have the leg looked at. Sadly, I'm starting to get used to that place. After a couple miserable hours waiting, the news isn't good. The issue isn't a knotted muscle, but what Doctor Lunzer calls an osteosarcoma – or a cancerous growth on the bone by my knee. Especially frightening are her words that immediate surgery is required just to "save the leg". I try to put on a brave face, but I am terrified. Save the leg? Is there I chance I'll never run again? And what if I refuse the surgery? Suddenly it hits me. There is another side to this equation – that saving the leg might be the first step in trying to save me.

When Doctor Lunzer leaves, I grab Dad's hand and squeeze with all I have. Then I lose it, burying my head into his chest and bawling.

Cancer sucks.

With surgery now set for the next morning, it is obvious that I won't be running in the county meet this weekend, and a faint voice whispers the haunting question in the backdrop of my mind - "will I ever run again"?

The next day that voice continues to echo in my head as they put me under for the surgery. Coupled with the worried expressions on Dad, Kara and Mom's faces, I drift off into an eerie trance, and begin to witness what I believe is my post-surgical future.

"It was a strange sight to see the doctor holding my leg in her hand – just dangling, like an appendage stolen from a mannequin in a window display. I wondered if the mannequin felt as hollow and empty as I did at that moment. It seemed that the new plastic, prosthetic leg I was about to receive,

would only end up being attached to the empty,
plastic figure I had become – stuck on display for all
to see. For all to pity."

Apparently I awoke from the surgery crying and screaming about an "empty plastic shell". This was one of those nightmares that, even though you are relieved to wake up from it, seems to cast a dark spell over you for the next several days, whispering to you that there were shreds of truth mixed within its haunting message.

During the recovery, I am never alone. After Dr. Lunzer stopped by to inspect her handiwork on my leg, there is a steady stream of visitors. Besides my family, Joey, Mom, and a few friends stop by from school bringing cards and telling stories about the recent meet. Even Coach Fitz dropped by to encourage me and tell me how much the high school track team needs me for the fall season. He had some students take videos from the weekend meet and post them to You-Tube, and during his visit we watched some of the videos on his iPad.

I smiled and thanked him, congratulating him on the team's success, but internally I wanted to upchuck. Forrest had claimed all three of the events that I had won last year. Though none of his finishing times would have beaten me, it was gut-wrenching watching him celebrate, and knowing the team won so handily without me. As much as Coach tried to reassure me, it seemed as if I wasn't needed at all – the team hadn't missed a beat without me. In fact, there was no mention of my name in any of the videos, even though I was the current record-holder in a couple of the events. The most difficult video to watch showed Kelly leaping on to Forrest's shoulders, like a fashion model hoisted in the air, a bright smile glowing over her beautiful face, after he crossed the finish line of the mile run. My race. My reputation. My girl. Gone.

I couldn't help wonder if the best was now all behind me. Would I ever break the four-minute mile? Would I steal 100 bases, or accomplish anything worth remembering? Had I just gone from "Dash" to "dud"?

Dr. Lunzer had warned me that I should expect to lose a significant amount of strength in the leg due to the surgery, and that there is even a remote possibility of a permanent limp. I'm not even going there. She underscored that recovery would be a long, slow process. "Slow" just isn't a welcome word in my vocabulary.

Joey stopped by again later that afternoon.

"Hey Dash. How ya doing Bro?

"Hey Joey. I'm okay. How are you?"

"I'm cool bro. Wanna play cards or a video game? Or are you too tired for another old-fashioned Joey butt-whuppin, domination of Dash?"

"Aw, Joey. You probably would win a few games with the shape I'm in. Ol' Dex just ain't feeling it right now?"

"Whoa Bro! What's up with all the black balloons flying in here? When did you decide to throw yourself a pity party and not invite me?"

"Huh?"

"Dude – I get your down, man. I got no idea what it feels like to be you right now. Fast as hell, smarter than everyone (except yours truly), and knocked down a bit by this cancer and surgery. But I have never known you to turn your back from a challenge. I have never seen you throw in a towel, and I have never heard you call yourself 'Dex'. What we have here is definitely a pity party. Now I'm gonna pop me some of these black balloons decorating the place, and get down to business."

"Business?"

"Yeah dude. We need to come up with a plan. How Dash beats the Dope and gets the girl."

"I don't follow."

"Sure you do. I know you well enough to know that what Dopey did at the meet this weekend is just killin you inside. I saw some of those You-Tube videos. There is no way you are gonna sit idly by while some goofball takes your spot in those races, and then lifts your secret crush up on his dufus shoulders. It's time we map out your training so you can get back on your feet and perform a modern David vs. Goliath...or in your case Dash vs. Gilligan."

I couldn't help myself. Joey's schmaltzy humor was just what I needed, and I burst out laughing.

"So your gonna help me take down Forrest?"

"Yep. Humpty takes a tumble. Dumbo goes down. It's gonna be an old-fashioned 'Thrilla in Vanilla'.

"You mean Manila, right?"

"Whatever, but vanilla tastes better. And..."

"And?"

"And...you get the girl."

"Kelly? How?"

"I have no idea. I still have to work on that part. Too bad you're not as cute as me."

Joey stayed through dinner, with his mom smuggling in a deep-dish from Geno's Pizzeria. We spent the afternoon playing games, (I don't recall him winning any of them) and brainstorming other fitting nicknames for Forrest to go with Dumbo, Dopey, and Dufus. Among the most memorable were "BI-MERV" which means *butthead in my rear-view*, and "UGOTNO" for *you got no class, you got no medals, and you got no Kelly!* Of course my personal fave was - "Dusty" as in *get used to eating my dust as I bury you in every race for the rest of your worthless pitiful life you big jerkwad*.

Exhausted from all the laughter, I needed a little shut-eye. Joey hit the road, promising to stop by tomorrow, and I closed my eyes picturing myself whacking no-class Dusty over the head with a prosthetic leg, with Kelly smiling by my side, her hand in mine.

Chapter 8

dash – (n): the mark or sign (-) to show the span in a series of numbers or years.

"Running for a Cure". I remember the large pink banners all over the 5K course that I ran one evening last summer with Dad. It felt good to know that my passion for racing was also helping some people who had cancer. I remember before the race there were some cancer survivors who spoke about their battle, the chemo process, losing their hair, riding an emotional roller coaster, and maintaining their resolve to beat this terrible disease. While I was inspired by the grit they demonstrated as they lined up to run, I didn't really appreciate the massive struggle they had gone through to get there. It seemed so foreign. So unrelatable. So "that'll never happen to me."

Throughout the course the roadside was marked with these small paper bags called luminarias that had a glowing candle inside and a message written on the outside. These glowing markers were dedicated to the memory of those friends and loved ones who fallen in the battle against cancer.

Dad had signed us up for the race because he had lost a dear colleague and friend from school to a rare form of the disease, and he wanted to run in her memory. I had only met Mrs. Hofler a couple times when I visited his school for different events, but I could tell she was one of those teachers that created magic in her classroom, because of how deeply her kids loved her. Dad said that in a era when teachers are pressured to focus on preparing kids for an onslaught of standardized tests, she instead intentionally fostered an environment where kids were encouraged to use their imagination, curiosity and natural creativity, and through that nurturing atmosphere they developed a passion for exploring the world around them that builds a foundation to become lifelong learners.

It was awkward writing a message in memory of Mrs. Hofler. I don't even recall exactly what I said, but I remember Dad's tears when he wrote his. After the race, we stayed for a ceremony that involved a wide array of speakers who shared memories of those who had fallen in the battle against cancer. We sat in a large section of students and staff members who had run in Mrs. Hofler's honor. There was a brother and sister who had both been students of hers that got up and shared. By the time they finished, there wasn't a dry eye in our group. What a testimony it was to her and how she impacted their lives.

Little did I know that night that I was soon running toward my own cancer. Perhaps I was even running with it at that time. Running towards cancer is an ironic thought. People run from cancer, not towards it. At least not intentionally. Maybe we just run, and cancer subtly attaches itself like a specter of fatigue during your race.

I have an appetite for the first time in several days, and my body doesn't feel like a boxer's sparring partner. Finally I may be on the rebound. With a serious case of bed head, I toss on my comfy Sox cap, and grab my pair of running shoes that Kara and Mom dropped off yesterday, as Dad and I make our way down to the hospital cafeteria to get a bite to eat. I am even tempted to jog down the hallway, but

Dad reels in my enthusiasm and insists on the elevator as transport downstairs. As I peruse all the menu items on display under the glass, everything looks like a lumpy mish mash of roller food from the local mini mart. My desire for food has disappeared. I can't stomach the fare. Finally I grab a small package of Oreos and nibble on those.

Dad grabs the paper and I find us a table near the windows. Though the ground-floor view here isn't necessarily appealing, at least I can see sun and sky. Beyond the full-to-capacity parking lot, lays a strip of trees. I imagine someone back there has to be running. Jealousy pangs me.

Dad scoots in his chair and prepares to snack with me. He only grabbed a bowl of soup, but I know he must be hungrier than that. He has hardly eaten the past several days. Out of habit, I remove my hat since Grandpa always insisted on hats off when we sat to eat. When I go to set it down, I notice the locks of hair falling from inside. Crap.

Now I understand why my head was tingling the other day. I hate to be so vain, and I know it's really petty given my circumstances, but I was so hoping to avoid any hair loss. Not that I was a teen heart-throb to begin with, but I always figured that my flowing blonde hair coupled with my speed had to have some measure of appeal. Now that I am limping, gawky and balding, I must look pathetic. Weak. Helpless. Slow.

Cancer sucks.

Dad tries to look over the box scores with me, but what is the point? I don't want to read about a bunch of healthy sports stars when I am stuck in some hospital with my hair falling out.

"Dash, what's up?" You don't seem interested in the box scores.

"Nah. I don't know Dad."

"Your stomach upset again? Is it the leg? Do you need to get some more pain medication?"

"Yeah. No. I don't know Dad."

"Son?"

Sigh. "Dad, look at my hat. My hair is..." My voice catches in my throat. I can't state the obvious.

"Oh son, Dr. Lunzer said to expect this. I'm sorry. I know it must really suck."

"Big Time! Dad, I'm falling apart. I just want to be back to normal. I just want to get out and run. Why is this happening to me?"

"I don't know son."

"I don't deserve this!"

"Nobody does, son."

"But why me?"

"Dash , there is no answer that. I wish I had answers, I wish I could take this away from you. Believe me, with all my being I do. I'd switch places with you in a heartbeat."

"No! I wouldn't want you to be sick either!"

"Of course not Dash. I wish I could take this from you. Son, I believe in you. You are a strong young man. You have always been a fighter. You have overcome some really difficult obstacles. You'll bring that same spirit to this fight."

"I don't feel like I'm putting up much of a fight right now. Can we go back to the room? I want to lay down."

I drifted off thinking about different obstacles I've faced. Challenges in training came to mind. Early defeats in middle school. Those were nothing like this. Of course Grandpa leaving was heartbreaking. And when he passed, I was devastated. But how do I get through this?

For some reason my mind wandered to "Dragon Hill." Located just a few blocks south of our school, Coach Fitz had used this natural monstrosity to whip his young runners into shape. The enormous, barren hill earned its' nickname because just a couple of attempts up left even our best runners' tongues dragging. Every Thursday after school we had to do hill repeats, sprinting up the steep mound as many times as we could muster. Coach used the hill to separate his dedicated core of runners from his cross-country wannabees. Even some of the strongest high-schoolers in our town couldn't hack Dragon Hill.

I was different. I enjoyed the challenge. Dragon Hill made me angry. Defiant. To me, the hill represented what Mom had done to us. Left us high and dry. Tried to hurt us. To break us. While most runners dreaded the hill, and fatigued after a few attempts, I reveled in the opportunity to conquer it. To me, it was "Dragon Jill", and there was no way I would ever leave that hill broken. Coach said that before I joined the team the record had been a mere five completions of the hill, and that particular kid did it only one time. Everyone thought it was a freak occurrence. I obliterate the Dragon, and have never left it without at least seven all-out furious sprints up and down its face.

Chemo is no Dragon Hill. It is a thousand times worse, and I feel overwhelmed. Sapped. Discouraged. Beaten.

I must have dozed off for a bit because I eventually realized that I was alone in the room. There were more cards along the window sill, and Dad's laptop was lying open on his chair, so he probably stepped out to make a few phone calls.

Cautiously, I ran my fingers through my hair, hoping that I it had stopped falling out and that most of it still remained. Wrong. Large clumps came drifting out with my hand, and I grab my Sox cap to hide the embarrassment. How pitiful.

Needing to pee, hospital rules say that I'm supposed to have someone help me to the bathroom, but I'm sick of feeling so feeble, so I wriggle myself in position to get up and drag my sorry butt over to the toilet. As I sluff across the room, I hear the various sounds from the hallway. Doctors and nurses carrying on casual conversations. A patient moaning a few doors away. Pain and agony and normalcy together. Sickness and suffering is commonplace here. I just want to go home.

While I never considered myself an artist or designer, whoever got the gig for these hospital bathrooms pulled a fast one. The tiles in here are the same color as the pee in the toilet, urine-yellow. What were they thinking? Any color would be better than this. In addition to the putrid wall hue, there are switches, dials, pull chains and buttons in here that are obviously meant to save a person in an emergency. Geez, that would be a horrible way to go – death on the potty.

As I sit here trying not to ponder all the doddering senior citizens who may have spent their last moments bare-bottomed on this very throne, I notice the bandages on my leg are loosened. The past few months I had admired how strong my legs were looking. Lean and muscular. Streamlined. Fast.

Since the surgery, I've been afraid to look. Will it be disfigured? Scarred? Gruesome?

Tentatively, I lift up the loosened wrap and notice the rainbow of purple, yellow, indigo and red on both the bandage and my leg. Yuck. Then I see what appear to be black lines within the pooling of colors near the incisions. Zig-zagging lines. Very black. These are obviously not my veins, but what are they? A toxic reaction to the surgery or the chemo treatments? Another disease? Trembling fingers lift the bandages higher until I notice the erratic lines create a pattern, a word.

Lunzer.

An autograph? My doctor friggin' autographed my leg? What was he thinking?

The cacophony of emotions is stunning, and draining. All at once I feel relieved, scared, angry, and depressed. I'm relieved that the black lines aren't some terrifying new manifestation of the cancer. I'm scared of the distinct possibility of being left so frail by this disease. I'm angry with myself for being so weak and afraid. I'm depressed because I feel like such a loser. I feel stripped down. Sapped. Vulnerable.

Cancer sucks.

Somewhere right now Forrest is probably running. Strong. With a stupid grin on his face. Thinking of Kelly. She is probably with her girlfriends shopping. Laughing. Smiling. Everyone else is moving on. Being normal. I'm stuck here between these walls of wiz feeling wimpy and wispy and wondering when I can get back to my own normalcy before everyone else has left me behind.

Screw these buttons and dials and emergency switches. I don't need help peeing or standing or washing or walking or anything. I hate being vulnerable. I'm done with needing. Defiantly, I hurl myself up, grab my robe, and angrily hobble down the hallway. It's time to go home.

The forty or so steps it takes to get to the elevator are more draining than any 800m race in my history, but I make it. Simultaneously exhausted and energized, I head down to the cafeteria to find Dad so we can go home. It tastes like freedom to be out of my room. I can't wait to smell the fresh air outside. To feel the sun shine down on my face. To hear something other than the beeps and bings of hospital gizmos surrounding me.

Making it to the ground floor, my escape attempt is successful thus far. I slowly shuffle my way through the tables and chairs looking for Dad. While nobody is specifically looking at me, it feels like they are all secretly *watching* me. Eyes peer around newspapers and magazines. Glances peek up from plates. Where is Dad?

Leaning against a table, I catch my breath and scan the room for Dad when I overhear one side of a phone conversation between an angry man and what I guess is his contractor.

"Jerry, how much longer is it going to be 'til my kitchen cabinets are delivered?

Seriously?

But the granite guys are supposed to be coming to measure for countertops tomorrow!

I have fifty people coming for a birthday party next week and my kitchen has to be finished! I don't have time for this! You'd better get those #@&%! cabinets installed today!"

Really dude? This guy has no grip on reality. He has party problems? I have CANCER! I can barely walk! I'm supposed to be the fastest kid in my school! His cabinets are going to be late? His party might be delayed? Want to trade?

He is in a hospital with sick, suffering people all around him, and is complaining about a hitch in his party plans? Something is seriously messed up here.

As I continued searching for Dad, I couldn't stop thinking about the party-pooper dude. He was so angry. Over a relatively small hassle. Stuck in his own little myopic world. Oblivious to the pain all around him. I began to feel sorry for him. And woozy.

With the room beginning to spin around me, I sat down and put my head on the table. After a few minutes, there was a gentle hand on my shoulder.

"Dash, what are you doing down here?"

"I was looking for you, Dad."

"Son, you're supposed to be resting in your room!"

"I just wanted to go home, Dad. I hate being here."

"I get it son. I want to take you home too. As soon as the doctor clears you to go."

A few minutes earlier, I would have fought to leave, but now feeling so sick and wobbly, I let Dad assist me back to my room, and my bed.

There is a gap in my memory of the afternoon, but I must have slept a bit again because when I wake up I am in a different room. It is still gray, but much smaller. There is no curtain divider. This is a private room. At least there are windows. Kara and Mom are here also. This is weird and unexpected.

"Dad, where am I?"

"They moved you to a different wing, son."

"Why?"

"This is a specialized section of the hospital. The staff here works specifically with cancer patients. They will be more familiar with your treatment needs."

"But how much longer do I have to be here?"

Never in my life would I have imagined what happened next.

My now very short life that is.

Tentatively, Dad sat on my bed. Kara nervously got onto Mom's lap. Then Dad delivered the crippling news. Between teary eyes and mumbled gasps, he took my hand and rendered the verdict – my cancer was terminal.

My days were now numbered.

How does someone process the news of their imminent demise? Especially when you considered yourself so young and invincible; full of dreams and goals and expecting your whole life ahead of you? I felt lied to. Cheated. Singled out. Robbed. Wasn't there some kind of universal promise made to kids my age that we had a reasonable life expectancy? Didn't I have a right to live out my high school and college years, and make a name for myself? What had I done to deserve such a malevolent sentence? Why was the creator of our universe stealing my life from me?

Dad, Kara and Mom tried to console me with words and hugs, but my die had been cast and I don't recall much of what they said. I felt lost and shell-shocked. Like a ghost, already half-departed.

In an attempt to cheer me up, Joey came over one afternoon later that week. I guess I was hoping that somehow his friendship could make me temporarily forget the bizzarro-reality that I had become a walking zombie with one bad leg already in the grave. I needed him now more than ever.

It was no such luck however. While he was just being typical, playful, charge-ahead Joey, I was in a dark place. The moment was awkward. It hit me like a ton of bricks when Joey suggested that I "*should make a wish list.*"

I know he meant well. I'm not sure what I would have said if the tables were turned and it was my best friend telling me that he just found out his cancer was terminal. Nothing I say will change his condition. There are no words to alter the inevitable.

"You should make a wish list. You know, like that Grant-A-Wish Foundation that helps kids like you realize their special dreams."

Kids like me.

Kids that are dying.

Joey began scribbling a list of possible ideas:

Throwing out the first pitch at a White Sox game.

Make sure they include clubhouse tour, premier club box seats, and

an autographed ball and jersey.

Sitting in the President's chair in the Oval Office.

Maybe signing a bill or two.

Riding with the Blue Angels at the lakefront celebration this summer.

Appearing on "Diners, Drive-ins and Dives" with the peanut butter & jalapeno sandwich being named after me.

I must admit, his ideas sounded pretty cool. I could imagine myself throwing out the first pitch at a real ball game, maybe even one televised on ESPN. Perhaps I could be a special guest in the booth during the game. That would be the thrill of a lifetime, wouldn't it?

Would it?

I guess I already had many "thrills of a lifetime." I had a collection of autographed baseballs from my favorite players. I had flown in an army helicopter with Grandpa. In fact, I had the world's coolest Grandpa who took me under his wing and taught me about some of the greatest sports heroes who ever lived. I had an amazing Dad who would give anything to switch places with me so that I could be healthy again. He always told Kara and I how proud he was of us, making us feel like we could accomplish anything. And yeah, I had a sister who although she could be pretty annoying, also could be really fun to be with, and I knew that she loved me. If the doctors couldn't give me any more time, what else could I really want?

Life was the only wish I could think of.

Chapter 9

dash — (v): to mix by adding another substance

Over the next few days I found myself spending a lot of time wishing. Not so much about cool ideas for some foundation to promote an awareness of my cancer, but about waking up from this nightmare. I couldn't shake the feeling that somehow I was incarcerated in a terrible dream, and I was desperate for some tool to break through these walls and make my escape back to the land of the living.

One moment, I had been the fastest kid in my school, full of strength and promise, and training to break the tape on a 4:00:00 mile. The next moment, I am lying in a hospital ward for terminal cancer patients, trying to figure out how to escape a very different, and very morbid, finish line.

No matter how much I wished to edit my story, the fact that I was entombed in a ward among incurable souls supplied the constant message that my days were dwindling. Each time I ventured into the hallways, I envisioned the other patients wearing race bibs, this time their numbers representing the amount of days they had left to live. I couldn't make eye-contact with them, instead keeping my gaze on the sanitized floors, for fear I might somehow see how many days remained for each of them. I was sure their bib numbers were all just double-digits. Or less.

How many days did I have? While a low race bib number usually reflected your status as an elite runner and was therefore a treasured commodity, I now yearned for a larger number. An endless number, like the irrational ones we learned about in algebra that kept going and going. An irrational wish for an irrational number. I didn't want life to end. I had way too much that I still wanted to do, and none of it belonged on a wish list.

As I sat in my room that in just a few short days had filled up with cards, race shirts, posters and other tokens from friends, relatives and well-wishers, I pondered over what I was going to do with my unknown amount of remaining days. I was clutching the bronzed shoes from Grandpa that Mom and Kara had brought over, (along with my prized collection of autographed baseballs that now were displayed across the windowsill), when I heard a gentle tap on my door.

"'Scuse Me. May I come in?"

Dad's cot lay next to my bed, between me and the door. He had been staying here 24/7 with me until the doctors would release me. Even though they had determined my cancer was terminal, they needed me to stay in the hospital a few more days to monitor the cancer and address my pain. The plan was for me to be able to spend whatever time I had left at home. Dad was pretty scruffy looking when he got up this morning, and he had just left the room to go clean himself up a bit.

The voice at the door was definitely young, and definitely female. Surely not a hospital employee.

"Hello? Is it okay to come in?"

Her kind face peered around the door, with a bright smile, radiant blue eyes, and an ill-fitting wig.

"Hi there. I'm Paige. I'm just a few doors down in room 207. I wanted to come over and say hello. Can I come in?"

"Um, sure. Hello."

"I hope I am not intruding. I noticed you came to our floor a few days ago and thought it might be nice to introduce myself."

"Thanks. That is nice of you."

With two hands gripping a walker, she stepped across the doorway, wearing footie pajamas and an oddly festive pair of fuzzy, multi-colored slippers that looked a few sizes too big for her feet. She had a sweet, kind voice that sounded as if it belonged to a much stronger girl than the frail silhouette before me.

"So you are...?" Her voice drifted off, as if she didn't know how to finish asking what was obviously on her mind.

Her words hung in the air and though I thought the question seemed kind of rude, I answered her anyway, figuring she might lack some of the common social graces.

"Yes, I am terminal. That is why I am here."

"Huh? Oh, I apologize! That's not what I meant. I was asking what your name is."

Doh! I'm such an idiot!

Chuckling for the first time in a long while, I began to feel a tiny renewal of normalcy. Maybe this cancer didn't have to define me. Maybe I could still be kind of like a regular kid.

"I'm sorry my name is Dash. Let me move this cot so you can come in."

"Dash? Your parents named you Dash?"

Chortling to herself, Paige ambled over and sat next to me as I explained the origin of my beloved moniker.

"Oh, so you are fast, huh? That's what all the race paraphernalia in here is all about, huh? How did you come to love running? Are your parents runners?"

I appreciated how she used the present tense when describing me as fast, talking to me as if I was still alive. Still important. Still valuable.

"Well, my Dad is a runner. It has always been one of his passions. We run together on the weekends in the forest preserve by our home."

"What about your mom?"

"What about her?"

"Is she a runner?"

"No. Her passion is music."

"Is she a singer, or does she play an instrument?"

"She's a saxophonist."

"Do you play an instrument also?"

"No. My parents had me take some piano lessons, but it wasn't my thing."

"So you share your dad's passion for running. What do you share with your mom?"

"Not much, really."

"Oh. Okay. Hey, what's up with all the balls on the windowsill?"

"That is my autographed baseball collection. My grandpa started it for me."

I was happy to change the conversation. I didn't want to talk about *her*. With my nerves calming down, I showed her the prized signatures from Jeter, Ventura, Yaz, Santo and Clemente. It was readily obvious that Paige didn't know much about the career accomplishments of most of these players, except for Santo and Ventura, who had spent the bulk of their playing days in Chicago. She wasn't interested in batting titles won, golden gloves amassed, or World Series rings. Yet she did seem to have a keen interest in their individual characters, asking about what they did outside of the game and what types of obstacles they had to overcome to achieve their dreams. She knew about Santo's battles with diabetes; how Roberto Clemente devoted much of his offseason time to helping people in need, eventually losing his life on a trip to deliver relief supplies to earthquake victims in Managua. She was familiar with the stories of Ventura developing lifelong relationship with cancer patients. She reminded me a lot of grandpa, with her primary interest being the character of the athlete.

"I'll be right back. I want to show you something."

As she left the room, I wondered what it was that she wanted to show me. Moreover, I wondered what her story was. Why was she on the same floor as me? What was her illness? How long did she have? And how do I even ask such questions?

Returning a few minutes later, she slowly approached my bed, her body creaking with each step. As her hands lifted toward me, my eyes fell to the box in her grasp. It was a vintage rectangular tin box, pocked and dinged over the years, with a beautiful patina.

"Here you go."

As she set the box in my hands, one of the nurses abruptly came in searching for my mysterious guest.

"Paige, what are you doing in here? You were supposed to meet with me for PT fifteen minutes ago."

"Oh, I'm sorry Anne. I'm coming now."

Cradling the box, I was mesmerized by the joy scrawled across her face as she left the room. How could she have been smiling, when she was so obviously weak and frail? Didn't she grasp the situation? Wasn't she aware that her number was nearly up? Everyone else in this area of the hospital moved with a somber gait, as if they were already gathering for a visitation service. Yet this girl carried a perplexing radiance.

It was several minutes before my tentative fingers decided to open the box. What could she have brought? She didn't even know me.

The tin container had a peculiar heft to it. It felt as if the object within had the desire to roll freely, but was hemmed in on all sides by some type of soft packaging. A ball? Could it be? But she had just learned that I collected them. Lifting the lid, I glimpsed at the familiar crimson stitching zippering the seams. I inhaled deeply, enjoying the comforting scent of worn cowhide. Scribbled across the side I noticed a somewhat faded autograph. I hesitantly lifted the beautiful gift. The first initial was unmistakably a "J", but the last name was written with flourish of loops and lines. Some ballplayers were notoriously worse than doctors, with their handwriting resembling some form of hieroglyphics. But I was accustomed to the challenge, and determined to crack this code. Decrypting the letters of the last name, I discerned that the combination of three intersecting petal-like loops formed an elaborate "A", which was followed by three smaller ovals, the first two having miniscule stems on their upper left.

Finally, the last two letters appeared to be the double consonant "tt". Assembling all these clues, "Abbott" emerged as the likely last name.

Whoa.

There had been many players with the surname Abbott over the years, but there was one that was especially near and dear to my heart. I remember grandpa telling me the stories about Jim Abbott, who was born without a right hand and yet pitched in the major leagues. He had a distinguished career, winning an Olympic gold medal, and even throwing a no-hitter for the Yankees. More than anything, he inspired millions by overcoming the tremendous obstacles that faced him. Another one of grandpa's character guys.

I was dumbfounded. Who was this girl, and why had she given me such a wonderful gift?

The longer I sat there, the more I began to feel an intense mixture of emotions.

First, tenderness, that someone could be so thoughtful. Then, my mood darkened. I felt guilt. And anger. I was guilty that she was smiling while in such obvious pain, and I had been wallowing in self-pity.

How could she have been smiling? Was it just the medication dulling her pain?

I was angry that she was smiling, and angry that she made me feel so guilty.

I felt guilty for being so angry.

I wondered which was worse, the cancer that was destroying my cells, or the emotions that were searing my heart?

As I sat confused in my bed, the nurse came in to check on all my tubes and machinery.

"I see you had a visitor. Did you like meeting Paige?"

As I drifted off, I thought about her. Paige. The mysterious girl who just entered my life. A soft, powerful essence drifting into my cold, dreary days. Why did I feel like I had just been sucker-punched?

She left a gift. A kind, thoughtful memento of her visit. I should have been happy. Moved. But a very different set of feelings stirred within me.

I am such a jerk.

Dad came back as I was struggling to digest my conversation with Paige.

"Hey son. I hope you don't mind that I stepped out. I needed to clean up a bit. I'm not sure if you noticed or not, but I was starting to feel odiferous and worried that I might be offending other people in the wing."

Normally I would join his playful banter, but I was still trying to make sense of Paige and her gift.

"Dad, I had a visitor".

"Really? Was it Joey? Or did your mother drop Kara off while I was gone?"

"No Dad. A patient from down the hall stopped by. A young girl named Paige. She gave me this."

"Oh my. A baseball? How did she know you collect them?"

"She came by and we talked a bit. After I showed her my collection, she went to her room and got this."

"Why did she give it to you?"

"I'm not sure. She had to leave for a PT session with a nurse before we had the chance to talk about it."

"Wow. That is pretty amazing. Tell me about the ball."

"Look at the autograph, Dad. Do you know who this is?"

He paused for a few moments, trying to decode the loops and lines just as I had a few minutes earlier.

"J. Abatte? J. Amonte? J. Acosta? I'm having a hard time making out the last name."

"It looks like Abbott to me."

"Whoa."

"Right."

"Wow, son. Grandpa would be stunned. That was one of his guys."

"Yeah. I was thinking the same thing."

With that, Dad grabbed a photo of Grandpa that he brought from home and placed it over on the sill by the baseballs. It was a photo of Grandpa and I at a Sox game. He had his arm around me, with that big warm smile of his. I remember his scent, like a musky cologne, and his patient gravelly voice that was always so reassuring. It was like he was here with me. In the hospital. Where I wouldn't come visit him because I was too afraid. Where he died, alone.

I couldn't stop the tears that followed.

"Dash, what is it? Why are you crying?"

"Dad, I am such a coward."

"That's not true son! Why would you say such a thing?"

"Grandpa – he died here all alone. Because I was too afraid to come visit him!"

"Dash, your grandfather understood what you were going through. He didn't need a hospital visit to know how much you loved him. You didn't hurt him. You weren't a coward. You just needed to process some things."

"No Dad, grandpa needed me, and I wasn't there for him."

"Dash, he understood. You not being ready to visit him didn't change his love for you at all."

"But Dad, I loved Grandpa so much, and I couldn't muster up the courage to come here and visit him! This girl Paige, a complete stranger, has more than enough courage to come visit me - a person she had never even met before! And she leaves me this incredible gift!"

"Oh son, that's 'apples and oranges'. Paige is a patient here, and undoubtedly has a very different perspective on life than you had when you were trying to work out your emotions after your mom left and Grandpa moved out."

"And another thing; Grandpa didn't die alone."

"He didn't?"

"No son. I came here as often as I could. And he had a cot next to his bed just like the one here."

"But Dad, you didn't sleep here when Grandpa was in the hospital. I remember you coming home and being with me and Kara."

"No son, I didn't sleep here. Your mother did. She was here every day and every night. She was by her father's side up to the end."

"Really?"

"Yes, son. Of course she was. I know you were really hurt by what she did, but your mother has a good heart. She loved her father very much and was devastated when he passed. I think that was one of the reasons she moved back here."

"I thought she was still in New York with her music when Grandpa was here."

"No son, she came back as soon as Grandpa was admitted here. She dropped everything to be with him. Didn't you read the letters she sent you?"

"no."

"You didn't? Seriously? Oh, Son."

"I'm sorry, Dad. I didn't know."

"Dash, as hard as it might be to understand this, your mother loves you. She knows she made a terrible choice, but she has been trying to fix that for a long time. She really hurt our family, no doubt about that, but she also hurt herself in the process. I've made my peace with that, and accepted it. I think Kara has also. I hope you find a way to also, Son."

I wasn't sure if I had it in me to make me peace with her, or how to do so even if I wanted to.

Chapter 10

dash – (n): spirited action; élan; vigor in action or style

Runners have a weird co-dependency with their watches. We are constantly checking them, monitoring our running pace, the distance we have covered, our location, and ultimately, our self-worth. The watch is the first item on after a shower, and the last item off before bed, if I remember. A runner's watch stores all his data, so he can chart his progress over time and tweak his training to meet his goals. Runners are obsessed with time.

As I sit with Joey, Kara, Mom and Dad sardined into my room, the reality hits me hard that I am no longer a runner, because I cannot bear to look at the time. I have stopped wearing my watch, and avoid looking at the clock. Time is a constant reminder of what I used to be. Now time has become the runner, running away from me quickly.

I can't watch.

We tried playing a few card games together, with Mom, Kara and Joey squeezing together on the cot across from Dad and I sitting on my bed. Cards used to be serious competition, no matter whether we played poker, spades, or rummy. Scores were kept, and bragging rights were fought for. There was usually laughter in the air around one of the Hamilton card games.

Now the air in the room was as sterile as the hospital we were connected to. Nobody laughed. Nobody really wanted to play; we just didn't know what else to do to pass time. And it was passing too fast for my comfort.

We tried making small talk, between Dad having to go out into the hall frequently to meet with doctors, and a few texts from friends on the track team. Joey asked if I had come up with any more ideas for the "Grant-A-Wish" list, but when Kara glared him down with appalled laser beams, he decided to drop the subject and zip his pie hole.

Trying to switch gears, Mom piped in "Dad tells me you had a guest the other day."

"Yeah. A girl down the hall stopped in to say hi."

"Dad said she gave you an autographed baseball?"

"Yeah. Check this out. This one is signed by a player that Grandpa loved."

I wiggled around the cot to the windowsill and handed the ball to Mom, who knew how much her dad treasured the sport of baseball, and how he cherished some of the game's heroes.

"Who is this, Dash?"

"His name is Jim Abbott. He was an amazing guy who was born with just one hand, but went on to pitch in the Olympics and eventually in the major leagues. He won an Olympic Gold Medal and even threw a no-hitter with the Yankees. Grandpa used to talk about him a lot!"

"Why did she leave you the ball?" Kara asked.

"I'm not sure. She got called away by one of the nurses before I had a chance to ask her."

"Have you talked to her since then?" asked Kara.

"Um, no."

"Do you know what room she is in? We could go visit her." Joey said.

"Yes...I mean no. I know what room she is in, but...but, visit her?"

"Sure. Why not?" Kara asked.

I wanted to say because I don't even know her. And she is sick. And dying. But it sounded so idiotic in my own head that I couldn't even mouth the words.

"Yeah Dash. Let's go see if she is in her room." Joey replied.

"Now?"

Before I knew what hit me, Kara, Joey, and I were walking down the hall to room 207.

God, I hated this place.

The door was ajar, so Kara politely knocked on it. Then she turned to me, with a frightened look on her face.

"Oh my goodness! I forgot to ask you! What is her name?" Kara gasped.

"Paige."

Kara knocked again. "Hello?"

Beyond the door, we could hear the jostling of creaks and squeaks as someone inside was slowly and painfully scrambling around.

"C'mon in."

Kara pushed the door open revealing a very cold, and very empty, room.

Paige was sitting against her bed, her hands pulling down the sides of her wig like a swimmer pulling on their swim cap.

"Wow I have visitors! Hi Dash! Hi unknown strangers! Welcome to my humble abode!"

I couldn't help but notice the stark contrast between her room and mine. Over the past several days, my room had filled with balloons, cards, and posters from family and friends. Her room was essentially barren, with the exception of a couple cards and a handful of worn books on her windowsill. Yet when she greeted us, her joyful smile immediately brightened the room like the sunrise at dawn, washing color and warmth over all of us.

"Hi Paige. I was just showing my sister Kara and my friend Joey the wonderful baseball that you left me, and we wanted to come down and say hi."

"Nice to meet you Kara. Nice to meet you Joey. You mean 'up', don't you Dash?"

"Huh?"

"You said that you came 'down' to my room. But I am in room 207, and you are in room 201. Doesn't that mean you had to come 'up' to my room?"

"Hmmm...you got me. I guess you're right."

"Oh Dash, I like this girl already. She is a clever one!" Kara exclaimed.

"Well let's see, I'm not used to having guests. I only have one chair, and the bed. Kara, why don't you sit here with me, and Joey and Dash can share the chair. I'll let you guys figure out who has to sit on who's lap."

Kara leapt on the bed, giggling, while Joey grabbed the chair leaving me standing on my own like I just lost a semi-final round of musical chairs.

"So we were wondering about the ball. How did you get it?" I asked Paige.

"It was a gift from Stan the Man." replied Paige.

"Stan Musial?" I asked.

"Who? No. Well I don't think his last name is Musial. Stan is one of my friends from the senior wing here at the hospital. He used to be a baseball coach and has a small collection of autographed balls just like you do. He gave this to me because he said I inspired him like one of his favorite baseball players, Jim Abbott who was born with just one hand but went on to pitch in the major leagues. He and Mudge always call me Paige Abbott."

"Mudge?" I asked.

"Hah! Yeah, she is another one of my friends from the senior wing. Oh, Mudge! Her real name is Margaret, but she got the nickname 'Mudge' from the word curmudgeon, because she is quite the cantankerous one! Most people think she is an old witch, but she is really just layers of barbed wire covering a velvet heart. Many layers. She is a hoot!"

As Paige went on about Stan and Mudge, I couldn't help thinking about Grandpa, who must have lived on the same senior wing. I wondered if he made any 'friends' while he was here. Did he meet Stan or Mudge? I also wondered what his room looked like.

Was it barren like Paige's? I hadn't even sent him a card while he was here!

"So you're not used to getting many visitors?" Joey asked.

"No, not really. Long story. In a nutshell, I have lots of families, but no real family." Paige stated.

An awkward pause hung briefly while we waited for her to clarify that concept.

"Let's just say that I have had a different journey than most kids. I'm not quite sure what happened to my original parents, but I have lived with a handful of different foster families over the years. I think my health issues have always overwhelmed them, and I would eventually wind up back in the hands of the state. There is one sweet woman, Mrs. Evelyn Crump, who has adopted me into her heart (if not legally on paper), and makes the hour-long trek from Rockford to visit me every few days. She has several small kids at home, but she does what she can to look after me. These past several weeks I have had my friends in the senior wing, and in my books."

Paige gestured to the handful of books on the windowsill.

"With being moved in and out of homes over the years, it was hard to keep any close friends. But books, and some of the extraordinary characters within their pages, have always been a constant for me. Some of my best friends are books. And since I have been here, Stan and Mudge have become my newest family. I make my way over to the senior wing whenever I can to hang out with them. Their space is more fun than this one, obviously. They even have shuffleboard!

"Can I see your books?" Asked Kara.

"Of course!" Paige glimmered.

Kara, like Dad and I, was quite the reader. At least when she wasn't bellowing along with her iPod that is. Since Kara was five years old, Dad made a habit of taking her out on Sunday evenings for a "date night". He told me that he wanted her growing up knowing how precious she was, and how she should expect a man to treat her when she was old enough to start dating. Sometimes it was a walk, or a bike ride. Sometimes it was a fancy restaurant. But I think most often, it involved time spent in the local bookstore, sharing a mutual love for reading. Looking back, now I understand why it seemed like she sang the most on Mondays.

Her eyes brightened as she reviewed the titles on Paige's shelf.

"Oh my goodness! You have some of my favorite books! *Jeremy Fink and the Meaning of Life!* This is one of the best stories! My Dad couldn't stop crying when he read this book!" Kara exclaimed.

Really? I didn't know that.

"And isn't Lizzie a riot with her kleptomaniacal ways!? She is part bravado, part teen-girl insecurity. I love that girl!" chimed in Paige.

Joey and I just exchanged glances as the girls chattered away.

They spent a few minutes discussing that story and the other books, along with their beloved characters and some of their favorite parts of each story. I was familiar with a few of the titles, but my ears really perked up when Kara read the last one, *The Miraculous Journey of Edward Tulane.*

"Oh, that is a new one in my collection. One of the nurses brought it to me a few days ago. She said she found it in the hall." Paige said, winking at me.

She knew?

"Mrs. Danielson read that to us in third grade" shared Kara. It was soooo good! Remember how Edward was so funny in the beginning, when he was admiring his own reflection in the window?"

"Yes! And how about when he was brought home by the old sailor, and the sailor's wife put Edward in a dress and named him Susanah!" chortled Paige.

"Didn't Pellegrina kind of creep you out though?" asked Kara. "She was always so dark and gloomy."

"Ha! I was thinking that Pellegrina reminds me a lot of Mudge! Hey, speaking of Mudge, why don't you all go to the senior wing with me to meet her and Stan? You'll love them!" said Paige.

"I'm not sure if I want to meet someone if she is like Pellegrina!" said Kara.

"Me either." Joey said.

"Oh come on. She only comes across a little rough. She really has a great heart." exclaimed Paige.

"Yeah, if we can survive that layer of barbed wire." Joey said.

"Okay! I'm in. We just need to tell Mom and Dad where we are going. Joey, can you walk me back to Dash's room real quick so I can explain this to my parents?" said Kara.

"Sure. Be right back guys." said Joey.

Great. Now it seems like we are going to visit the senior wing. The place where Grandpa was when he passed. I hadn't even wanted to come down here and see Paige. But I guess that I am glad we did. I'm happy she got to meet Kara and Joey. She seems to really enjoy them. But am I really up for this?

"So from the little wink you gave me I guess you figured that was my book. But how did you know?" I asked.

"Well, it has a personal note written on the inside cover. To someone named 'Dash'. I'm no rocket scientist, but I figured there can't be too many people with such a cool moniker as that. Here, you can have your book back." Paige offered.

"No! ... I mean, no thanks." I said. "You can keep it. I want you to have it."

"Are you sure?" she asked.

"Yes." I stated in relief.

After Joey and Kara returned, we began to make our way down to the senior wing. With Paige creaking along, Joey grabbed a wheelchair from the hallway.

"How about a lift?" he offered.

"Do you have a license for this?" asked Paige.

"Yes Ma'am. I earned it the old-fashioned way. I got it in the bottom of a cereal box." Joey smirked.

"Then onward we go!" cheered Paige.

Chapter 11

dash – (n): a short race

"I – 31." a snarky voice croaked.

"Get up and run!" responded the delighted blue-haired crowd.

Nervously pushing open the doors of the senior wing, I had expected to see a dreary group of geezers bent over in their wheel chairs; sputtering and muttering and dozing and drooling. I assumed it would be rather depressing. Instead, it was awkwardly festive, like walking in to a busy bingo parlor on a Friday night.

A couple dozen seniors were gathered around a smattering of tables embroiled in a competitive bingo match. Sure, some of them were drooped over, and the smell in the room had the unpleasant mixture of cheap perfume with a tinge of retro subway bathroom, but I was struck by what else was in the air. Something that was much lighter than the air in

my wing. Something that almost resembled...
happiness. Or contentment.

Instead of the creeping presence of death, there was an abundance of the opposite. I was engulfed in life.

"G – 54." The bingo lady snarled.

"Clean the Floor!" was their playful reply.

There was a parlay back and forth between the collection of seniors and a portly old woman with coke-bottle glasses sporting a dew rag bandana like she was the crotchety queen bee of a retired biker gang. The Harley-Davidson Grandma looked as if it had been a long time since she last rode a chopper, and her grimacing facial features made it seem like it had also been a while since she had her own set of mandible choppers.

"B – 9," cried the motor mama.

"Doctor's orders!" was the choral refrain.

While the secret lingo of the bingo universe continued on, a brawny man with salt and pepper hair noticed our entrance.

"Hiya Paige! Who have ya rustled up with you? C'mon over here."

His curly locks were bustling from beneath a tattered navy blue baseball cap with a cursive grey D emblazoned on it. He had a barrel chest and leathery skin, approaching us with a loud clip-clopping sound produced by a pair of fluorescent teal flip-flops, apparently engineered out of duct tape. He had warm blue eyes that conveyed a blend of wisdom and sadness. Looking into those eyes, I couldn't help but see Grandpa.

"N – 41."

"Life's begun!"

"BINGO!"

A younger male nurse wheeled the winning patient up to the biker granny to have his card checked for accuracy.

"It looks like Ray's lucky streak continues, huh Stan?" Paige said to the kind man who was ushering us back to his table.

"Yeah. He has been on a heater all month long! So who is this crew you brought with you today, Paige?" The man replied.

"Stan, I made some new friends today. Real flesh and bones this time! Not just friends from the pages of my cherished books. Let me introduce you. This is Kara, Joey and Dash."

"Nice to meet you Karen, Joey and Dan. How do you all know Paige?"

"No Stan." Paige corrected in a louder tone. "It is Kara, not Karen. And this is Dash, not Dan. Dash is just a few doors down from me. Kara is his sister, and my race-car driver here, Joey, is their friend."

"Well, nice to meet each of you. Any friend of Paige is a friend of mine. All of ours, really." said Stan. "Can I get you each a bingo card or two?"

"Deal me in!" Joey exclaimed.

"Me too!" replied Kara.

"You know I'm good for a couple cards" grinned Paige. And grab a couple for my buddy Dash here too. I need to school him in the fine art of bingo."

As we scooted our chairs in around Stan's table, gathering bingo cards and plastic chips to mark our spaces on the card, I noticed that Stan was using little origami birds as his bingo card markers. The little creations came in a variety of colors, but each had been constructed with the same fluorescent duct tape that formed the sandals on his large feet.

"Hey Mudge, we have some newbies here. How about sending some good mojo this way?" Stan pleaded with the biker lady.

"They can wait their turn like the rest of the old farts in here, Stan. Let 'em pay their dues, man!" the old lady snarled.

"Dues? I thought bingo was a free game" Joey remarked.

"Don't worry son. She isn't referring to money. She means paying the price of admission to the senior wing – you know, all the fun stuff that comes after you reach senior citizenship: hair and teeth falling out, memory loss, wrinkled faces and big ol' diapers. *Those* dues. The bingo game is free. Ol' Mudge just lives with a chip on her shoulder and likes to remind our guests that being a resident in our lovely wing has an enormous price tag."

That quieted Joey, who was probably thinking about those layers of barbed wire.

"Now don't mind Mudge. She can be pretty off-putting to the people who don't know her, but she grows on you after a while" declared Stan.

As we played a handful of bingo rounds, Paige prompted Stan to tell us a little of his story. Apparently he used to be the baseball coach for Dutchinson, a small college in eastern Pennsylvania that was one of the first colleges established after the revolution. His teams won several conference championships while he coached there, and a couple of his players even had a stint in the pros.

"You must be real proud of your accomplishments there" asked Joey. Were they called the Tigers? That hat kind of reminds me of the Detroit Tigers.

"No. This hat is from De LaSalle. I moved here to start a baseball program for the area community college" chimed Stan.

"How did your team fare at De LaSalle?" I asked.

"They were perfectly awful! Gosh, we had no talent whatsoever. We didn't even win a game the first three seasons! It was the best time of my life." beamed Stan.

He went on to tell us how all the championships he won at Dutchinson didn't give him the joy that the startups at De LaSalle did. It turns out he was a great coach, but a miserable person when he was at Dutchinson. He was so consumed with winning and forging a successful reputation, that his ambition drove everyone he cared about away. He lost his marriage, and any connection with his two sons, because he couldn't see past his own goals. Even the players that he poured his energy into had no real relationship with him. De LaSalle provided a second chance, and a different perspective.

I wonder if my own ambitions have pushed people away. Joey has always stuck by my side, even when I've been all wrapped up in my races and goals. But could he say the same about me? What other people tried to befriend me, only to be driven away by my all-consuming push to make a name for myself? Had I passed up flesh and blood friends for ribbons, medals and trophies?

An elbow to the ribs brought me out of my fog. "Dude, you have a bingo! Call it out!"

"Bingo for the newbie!" Paige shouted.

"Well tell your newbie boyfriend to drag his sorry butt up here and prove it. This 'ol bat isn't getting any younger!" grumbled Mudge.

"Or any kinder." snickered Joey.

"What's that young man?" snarled Mudge.

"Careful Joey, bats have sonar" reminded Stan.

"Nothing, Ma'am." Joey said, as he slunk down into his chair.

I cautiously made my way up to have Mudge scan my card. I wasn't terribly interested in getting any prize; I just wanted to make it back to my seat in one piece. As she uncovered each of my squares, she mumbled something angrily under her breath. I couldn't make out much of it, but I think she said something about my being "too young."

"Excuse me?" I retorted.

"Hold yer horses, boy! I'm gittin yer prize."

"What were sayin to me?"

"I wasn't sayin anything to you. I don't even know you. Now take your winning card, and your ticket and git back to your table."

As I turned, I could have sworn she mumbled something about "dumb luck."

I'm not sure what Paige saw in her, but I was really starting to dislike her.

"Man, she is rough!" I moaned when I got back to our table.

"Are you sure she has a heart in there?" Kara whispered to Paige.

"How many cousins do you have?" Paige asked.

"Two. Why?"

"When are their birthdays?" Paige continued.

"I'm not sure, but what does that have to do with it?" Kara puzzled.

Paige leaned forward in her wheelchair. In a hushed tone, she exclaimed "Well, Mudge would never want me to tell you this, she is kind of like a warped version of Robin Hood. She doesn't have a penny to her name, yet somehow she is able to send out birthday cards to dozens of different kids she has met since she has been here. She calls them her "cousins", remembers all of their birthdays, makes the cards herself, and sticks a piece of gum in every envelope."

"But where does she get gum if she is penniless?" asked Joey.

"The word around here is that she has a habit of pocketing packs of gum from the hospital gift shop." chimed in Stan. "But don't worry, the staff knows about it, and where the gum is going. They tend to look the other way since they know the gum is going out to kids battling through cancer. Just don't tell Mudge. She likes feeling like she is getting away with something." he smiled.

"And she has all of those birthdays memorized. Not to mention her 'Mudge-Fudge' creations." said Paige.

"Huh? What do you mean?" asked Kara.

"Mudge is a wicked baker." whispered Paige. "On weekends, the seniors are allowed to do some baking in the kitchen. Each weekend, Mudge spends several hours hobbling around on two bad legs making a killer fudge recipe, usually combining ingredients that you wouldn't normally expect to work together, but it is always delectable. Mudge-Fudge is the best thing we eat all week! She growls and cusses when we conjure up some excuse to peek in the kitchen, but you can tell she loves how happy her fudge makes everyone."

"Wow! She does have a heart of gold!" Kara exclaimed.

"Hey, quiet down over there you annoying little pipsqueaks! This is the senior's wing and we enjoy our peace and quiet!" quipped Mudge across the room.

"There's that barbed wire." Joey carefully muttered.

I think Mudge heard him, because I noticed a devilish smirk cross her face.

After a while, Paige began to get really tired, so we decided to head back to our wing.

"Strap your seatbelt on Princess Paige, as I drive your carriage back to the castle." Joey proclaimed.

"Ooh! Nobody has ever called me a princess before! Better get a move on before you turn into a pumpkin."

Now it was my turn to elbow Joey, but he didn't seem to mind at all, other than his red face.

After dropping off Paige, Joey hung out in my room while waiting for his mom to come and get him.

"Did you guys notice how barren her room was? Except for her books, she has nothing. No balloons, no flowers, no cards. It was very sad." mentioned Joey.

"I know. I felt so bad for her. Yet it was pretty amazing how happy she seems to be." Kara noted.

I noticed how full my room seemed by comparison. It was pretty ironic. My room was full, but my heart felt empty. Paige's room felt empty, but her heart seemed full. There was something about her. She seemed to understand something, or know something that I didn't. I needed to find out what that was.

"I have an idea!" Kara declared. "Why don't we do like Mudge does? We could make cards for Paige, and other kids who are sick."

"That's a great idea!" Joey remarked.

Dad and Mom heartily agreed.

I nodded along, but felt awkward inside. It sounded like a charity project that was beginning, for kids like me and Paige. I knew it was a great idea, but it hurt inside at the same time, because I had the sneaking suspicion that those cards were going to last longer than Paige was.

And longer than me.

"Joey, we could each ask a bunch of our friends, and our classes to write cards to Paige. She would have tons of cards!" Kara said.

"We could even make it a school project! My mom was just telling me of a website called "chemo angels" where people send cards to chemo patients. Maybe our classes could do the same thing for patients here."

"Hey Dash, can you show me the cafeteria? I think I could use a coffee." Mom asked.

"Sure, Mom."

While I have spent the past several years avoiding any alone time with Mom, I just had to get out of the room. I wonder if she sensed how awkward I was feeling and decided to throw me a lifeline. I just hope this wasn't her attempt to corner me for one of her rants.

As we rode the elevator down to the ground floor, there was surge of tears welling up that I was unable to suppress.

Mom wrapped her arms around me.

I didn't have the strength to resist.

Her embrace is just like after I had broken the window when I was younger, except this time the shattering wasn't glass.

It was my heart.

Over the past several days, Joey and Kara have been with me at the hospital nearly around the clock. I'm sure Kara has special permission to miss so much school, given that her brother has a terminal illness. And I'm guessing that Joey's parents have finagled some kind of arrangement as well. I'm very grateful for their company.

We have spent most of our time hanging out with Paige, playing games, hearing ways that she identifies with her favorite book characters, and even occasionally venturing our way into the senior wing. We're getting used to Mudge's ornery temperament, as long as we can keep a safe distance. I have to protect the short time I have left. There is obviously a lot more than meets the eye with her, though. A few days ago Joey and I were working on my "Grant A Wish" list, down in the cafeteria, and Mudge came over to the table.

"What are you two miscreants working on?"

"I'm helping Dash with his 'Grant A Wish' list" Joey replied.

"Why waste your time with that list? We're all terminal, hon. Use the time for people you love, not things to get or do."

With that, she moved on.

It was like a punch in the gut.

Who was she to tell me how to use my last days? It's not like I had much to look forward to. I lost running. Lost baseball. Lost my reputation to Forrest. Lost any chance of having a girlfriend like Kelly. And I was losing the time on the clock. At least this list gave me something to look forward to. A last hurrah, so to speak.

Suddenly, it didn't seem very appealing.

Thanks Mudge. She was like a dark cloud. A real party pooper.

Stan however, was the opposite.

A couple days after the bingo contest, Stan stopped by my room with a gift. He had taken my winning bingo cards (I won a second time before we left), and cut out a pair of flip flops, reinforcing them with cardboard and duct tape. They were black, with silver pinstripes and a Sox logo on each sole. On the top of each sandal, the winning bingo cards were displayed. Beneath Mudge's highlighting of the winning combinations, Stan had inscribed a quote. It was from the great Jackie Robinson, but it was a quote that I wasn't familiar with:

"A life is not important except for the impact it has on others."

It wasn't that long ago that I had hopes of eventually being famous. I had wanted to make an impact. Now I wouldn't have the chance to have my name become synonymous with some great feat or accomplishment.

But was Jackie Robinson's legacy really all about his fame? Was his impact something that could be reduced to the back of a baseball card? Grandpa taught me better than that.

Maybe I won't be famous. Maybe I don't need one last hurrah. But I want to make a difference. I want my time to matter. Was Stan telling me that I could still do that?

"Thanks Stan. This is such a thoughtful gift. I love the shoes, and especially the quote."

After showing the shoes to Dad and Mom, I slid them on. They were surprisingly comfortable for a cardboard and duct tape creation cobbled together. They may not be too durable, but they mean as much as any pair of track shoes I own, except for the pair Grandpa had bronzed.

While Dad, Mom and Stan looked through my autographed baseball collection, I clopped out of the room in my new flip flops, summoning the courage to join Joey and Kara back in Paige's room. Over the past few days, she had been teasing me about how silly I was acting trying to hold on to the remnants of hair I had left after the chemo. I was wearing my ball cap wherever I went, embarrassed about going bald. Even my eyelashes were falling out. Paige encouraged me to make little eyelash wishes. I used the first couple wishing for more hair, then used the rest to wish for more time, for each of us. Meanwhile, Paige had stopped wearing her wig altogether. She was obviously fading, growing weaker and weaker physically, but she has decided to embrace the inevitable. Joey commented on how pretty she is, with or without her wig, which earned him a little peck on the cheek. In a show of support, for both Paige and I, he promised to bring his dad's clippers from home and get his head shaved today. Paige and I will be doing the honors, but I'm not looking forward to it. I know that eventually Joey's hair will grow back.

As I enter Paige's room, they are all set to go. I am amazed at all the cards, flowers and stuffed animals that decorate the room. Wow! Kara and Joey have been busy! There are well wishes from kids and parents all over town. There is even a banner hanging that was signed by the staff and students at our school. It has pictures of various book covers, highlighted by the books on her shelf. In bold letters it says: "Paige - A Friend of Books is a Friend of Ours".

Joey is seated in a wheelchair by the sink, and Paige is next to him, in her wheelchair, with the clippers plugged in and already buzzing.

"Ready to go, Dash?" Paige asks.

"Any last words for your follicles, Joey?"

"No buddy. I'm down with this. I'm going to make bald look good!"

"So Paige, do you want the left side, or the right side for Joey's chemo cut?"

"Let's have a little fun with this! How about a game of tic-tac-toe?"

"Definitely!"

As Paige, Kara, and I take turns mowing Joey's hair, Kara is happily singing away. In fact, she has been singing a lot around Paige, and it doesn't bother me anymore. We are getting along. It reminds of how things used to be before Mom left. I think about the simple joy I feel around Kara. Why have I wasted so much time before, in stupid arguments and fights with her? Maybe this is what Dad had meant when he asked me to learn to just enjoy her.

It turned out that Joey didn't look like anything but the loyal and courageous friend I have always known him to be.

I took a deep breath, and followed suit.

"Okay guys, I'm not letting Joey hog all the fun. Besides, if I'm going to be a cue ball anyway, I might as well show Joey how to make it look cool!"

"Dash, you want me to shave your head, too?" Kara asked.

"Yep sis. I'm ready. Let's do this!"

Dad entered the doorway.

"Me too, Son."

"Me three." I heard Mom say as she followed in.

Chapter 12

dash – (v): to hurry away; leave.

I have to give Mom a lot of credit. I didn't see that coming. After Kara finished buzzing my leftover hair, and I shaved Dad's, Mom sat down in that chair and asked me to cut her hair as well.

"Okay, Dash. My turn."

"But Mom, you might really regret this! Guys can handle being bald. It looks normal. I'm not sure women look right without their hair."

"Ahem" smirked Paige.

"Dude!" nudged Joey.

Open mouth, insert foot.

"I'm sorry. Paige, you look great. It's just that I have a hard time picturing my mom without her long hair."

"It's okay Dash. I want to do this. I am so proud of you, and I want to show you and everyone else that I am with you through this." Mom said.

Kara pulled her chair next to Mom's.

"Me too." she replied. "Now get cutting, bro."

Auburn locks and curls began falling to the ground in bunches. The pile gathering on the floor makes it look like Chewbacca has been shaving.

At first I'm nervous, as if somehow I might give them a bad hairstyle. But I soon find myself savoring this moment, slowly running the fingers on my left hand through Mom's soft and silky hair, ahead of the clippers that are in my right hand. I can feel her courage. Her strength. Her love. I remember running my fingers through her hair when she used to read stories to me at night. I remember her affection. I remember us being a family.

"It's feeling kind of chilly up there. How do I look?"

She never looked more radiant to me.

Kara then followed after her.

"Sis, you don't have to do this. I don't want anyone giving you a hard time at school."

"Dash, if anyone gives me a hard time I will sick Squirt on them. Or maybe Mudge. I want to do this. Now hush and get cutting."

As I re-started the clippers, she began singing "Girl on Fire"

"Everybody stands, as she goes by
Cause they can see the flame that's in her eyes"

Her voice never sounded sweeter.

Mom and Kara were amazing.

And while Mom didn't shed a tear when I shaved her head, I had noticed plenty of tears when she watched Kara shave mine. I know I need to talk to her. I just don't know where to start or what to say.

Over the next several days I spend most of my time hanging out with Kara, Paige and Joey. Paige is sleeping more, and her skin looks almost transparent. I'm not sure how much longer she can hang on. When she is awake, Joey is often holding her hand, and when he isn't, Kara usually is. When they have to go to school or home, I spend most of my time trying to figure out what to say to Mom. I'm really stuck with that one. Plus, I'm probably using that dilemma to avoid being alone with Paige. I'm not ready for her to leave yet. And I'm not ready for Mom to return.

As usual, Dad seems to read me. A few days earlier, he had brought in a ball and each of our baseball gloves. Today, he took me out to the patio, where we sat on benches across from each other and played a little catch. With my leg all wrapped up, I couldn't really move around, but it was one of the best games of catch we ever played.

"Son, I'm really proud of you. You have been so courageous through this whole ordeal."

"I don't think so, Dad. I feel just the opposite."

"How can you say that? I see how you have been so kind Paige, and you have really been working hard to get along with Kara, and even Mom. That is huge! Not to mention you allowing Kara to shave off your hair! You've been amazing!"

"But Dad, in all those things you mentioned, I was really just following someone else's example. Paige has been the kind one. She almost seems oblivious to her own condition, and is just so caring of everyone around her! As far as the hair, that was really Joey being courageous. I just felt embarrassed that I was being so chicken with the little bit of hair I had left."

Dad set the mitt and ball down and sat beside me.

"I understand son, and that is why I am so proud of you. Courage isn't the absence of fear. It is how you respond to your fear. You have stepped up. You've really grown into a brave young man."

He pulled me into a tight embrace and kissed my newly shaved head.

"Dad, I really appreciate your words, but I'm not sure they fit me. I still feel all messed up inside."

"Tell me, son."

"Where do I start?"

He took my hand.

"Gosh Dad, I feel so foolish. All I ever wanted was to BE somebody. You know, to do something special. I wanted to be famous somehow. And I look at some of the people here, like Stan, or Paige, and I wonder if any of that really matters. And I wonder what did I do with my life? What difference have I made? Here I am with this stupid cancer, and I still am afraid of the same things."

"Afraid of dying? But of course you are! We all are!"

"Yeah, dying. But more than that. I'm afraid of living without meaning, without purpose. I'm afraid that this cancer hasn't really taught me anything. I'm still afraid of the same things I've always been afraid of."

"Like?"

"Losing people. Mom left. Grandpa left. Now Paige is leaving. I can't even bring myself to go visit her room by myself. It's just like Grandpa all over again!"

"Son, look at me. I understand. Losing people is always really hard. But people leaving us doesn't mean they stopped loving us. Grandpa never stopped loving you. Paige's care for you won't change."

"I feel like I let Grandpa down. I didn't go see him when he was here. I was so afraid. Now I am letting Paige down."

"Grandpa always understood. He knew you loved him, and he never stopped loving you. I'm sure Paige will feel the same. I'm sure she is grateful for all the times you do visit her, whether it is with Joey and Kara, or by yourself. She knows you are her friend."

"What about Mom?"

"What about her?"

"I have been shutting her out for years. But I don't want things to end this way between us. How do I open up to her now? I don't know what to say to her."

"What do you want to say to her?"

"I don't know. I have been so mad at her, for so long. She hurt us so bad. But I can see she has really been trying, for a long time. You and Kara both seem to have made peace with her. I just don't know how to."

"I know she never stopped loving you, Son. And I know whatever you choose to say to her, she won't stop loving you now. You have a great heart, Son. You'll find the words. Like I said, I've never been prouder of you. You're so courageous. Your vulnerability here proves that even more. I love you."

Over the next several days, Joey, Kara and I spent as much time as we could with Paige. Sometimes Mudge and Stan were in her room also. Dad and Mom even joined us a couple times. We took turns reading some of her favorite books with her, getting to know her "friends" from her favorite stories.

"You know Mr. Hamilton, you remind me an awful lot of Jeremy's Dad, Mr. Fink, from one of these books."

"Why is that?" Dad asked.

"Well", Paige said with the most mischievous grin her weak body could muster, "let me say two reasons. One, he is a really great dad. And two, (she winked)... you HAVE to read the book."

With a snicker, she handed the book over to my dad, who hugged her tenderly, thanking her for being such a delightful friend to me and Kara.

"And you, Mrs. Hamilton, you remind me of Susanna." I didn't quite get the reference, but I could tell that Kara did as she gave Mom the biggest squeeze imaginable. Mom seemed to appreciate the comparison.

During one of our visits, Paige asked me whatever happened to the 'Grant-A-Wish-List' I had been working on.

"I don't know it just kind of fizzled."

"When I first came here, one of the nurses approached me about making a list also. I had a hard time figuring what to wish for. Then I explained the frustration to my friend Evelyn, who reminded me that it was okay to accept gifts offered by others who want to help. After talking about it, I realized the one thing I really wanted was some flesh and blood friends. That is why I started visiting the senior wing. And then I was granted my wish by meeting you, Kara and Joey."

"Wow, that is so cool!" Kara replied.

"Yeah." said Joey. "I helped grant a wish. Awesome!"

Later, after Joey and Kara had left, I mustered up the courage and went back to see Paige.

It was like she was expecting me.

"Hiya, Dash. How are you feeling tonight?"

"I'm okay. Just wanted to stop by and see how you were feeling."

"Come here, bud. I have something for you." Paige patted a spot next to her on the bed.

I sat beside her, realizing she looked a little stronger than she had in the past several days. She was actually sitting up on her own power.

"This really isn't much of a gift since it belonged to you originally, but I want to give it back to you anyways. I'm guessing either you didn't like the book, or you never read it."

I knew what was coming, but this time I didn't resist. She handed me *The Miraculous Journey of Edward Tulane.*

"Dash, what is one thing that you really want?" Paige gently asked.

"I don't know. I just want to make a difference. I want to know my time here helped somebody."

"Oh, you have made a difference already! Your sister thinks the world of you! Joey idolizes you. Your parents are so proud of you. And you granted my wish by being a great friend to me."

"Thanks. That really means a lot to me."

There was a quiet pause.

"Dash, what are you thinking?"

"It just feels like there should be something more. That there is something else I need to do."

"If there is, you'll know it when you see it." She nudged me with the book.

"Why do you want me to read this so badly?"

Paige had an impish glow. "Let's see. How did I answer your dad? Let me give you two reasons. One, he is an amazing character, and two..."

"I know, I know." I muttered. "I HAVE to read the book!"

"That's right, Edward" she grinned. "I think you still have a miracle or two on your journey."

By the time I got back to my room, I had an idea forming. A way to make a difference. I wanted to organize a race. I ran some ideas past Dad, and he loved the concept. Finally, I had a plan. Or the beginnings of one. It was a simple 5K race to raise people's awareness of Hodgkin's disease. I fell asleep feeling like I was on track to make a difference. That my journey would matter.

Paige's journey ended sometime during that night.

When Dr. Lunzer walked in the next morning, I could tell her visit wasn't about me. Or at least about my condition. She had been Paige's doctor also, and she saw our friendship develop over her many follow-up visits to each of our rooms. I could tell by the sadness in her voice that she had built a special relationship with Paige. But that was no surprise; Paige had that effect on all of us.

"I'm sorry to tell you this Dash, but Paige passed last night."

Dad held me close, but somehow I was already at peace. I think last night felt like our goodbye.

That day, Kara, Joey and I stopped by Paige's room one last time, but it had already been emptied and cleaned. Except for a couple books on the windowsill, each with a little note sticking out of the top. One was entitled Blood on the River and was addressed to Joey. The other book was called Out of My Mind and was left for Kara.

We quietly made our way down to the courtyard.

"I didn't really get to say goodbye." Kara mumbled.

"Me either." Joey said.

"I wonder if Stan and Mudge feel the same" Kara mused. "Maybe we could organize some kind of little memorial service here for her."

"That's a great idea, Sis! I think it would be a great way for all of Paige's friends to say goodbye." I put my plans for the 5K race on hold for now and started working on the details for the memorial service.

We gathered the following evening in the senior wing. Mudge had made a big poster with a collection of pictures of Paige on it. There was a sparse amount of early childhood photos. There was a picture of her with a baseball player. I looked closely and it was Jim Abbott, who had signed her ball. Most of the pictures were from her time in the hospital. Below the photos, was her name Paige Abbott, with the birth year and this year separated by a little hyphen. She had lived thirteen short years.

Originally I had expected a small service. Of course the seniors who reside in the wing would be there, along with staff members, Joey, and my family. We also made sure Evelyn was invited. Joey mentioned the memorial service at school. There was an outpouring of compassion from the people who had signed her banner. Apparently, many of them had been following Paige's journey though Kara and Joey. I was surprised at how many staff and students from my school came out. Suddenly, I felt self-conscious about the walker I had been relegated to these past few weeks. I think I looked as frail now as Paige did when I first met her. I was worried that my harrowing appearance would unnerve my classmates. They hadn't seen me since I had been admitted here, and I didn't want to frighten them. I needn't have worried. Soon I realized that Coach Fitz was there, with my whole team. Even Forrest. They all had their heads shaved.

Stan welcomed everyone, and shared a few words about his time with Paige. He told what an amazing, courageous and strong young girl she was. He shared that in his short time with Paige he learned more from her about how to treat other people than he had probably been able to teach all of his athletes in his years of coaching.

Mudge got up to speak, clutching a book that Paige had left for her, but then sat back down without saying a word.

Dr. Lunzer elegantly shared about the dignity and grace that Paige lived each day with.

As others took a moment to share their own memories, I looked at that poster with Paige and her photos. I looked at that little hyphen between her birth year and this year. That little dash that summed up her life between the numbers.

It was a short dash for her. A short race. But she made the most of it.

Coach Fitz and the team came by and huddled around me. Most of my teammates didn't know what to say, but just being there meant the world to me. Coach Fitz put his arm around me and told me what a champion I am and how proud he is of me. Then the team gave me a running singlet signed by all the team members. It was pretty touching. When they were leaving, Forrest made his way over and fist-bumped me.

"Dude. You're still the best runner our school has ever had. We're dedicating our season to you."

I didn't know the big lug had that in him. I was really moved. Maybe Kelly was in good hands after all.

When I got back to my room, I pulled out the book that Paige had left me. There was a card inside, telling me how proud she was of me. She thanked me, for helping to grant her wish. She thanked me for being a friend who saw past her cancer, saw past her loneliness, and became part of her journey. She reminded me that I was on a great journey of my own.

As I opened the book to begin reading it, I noticed the handwriting inside the front cover. I knew that writing anywhere. It was a note from Mom.

Chapter 13

dash – (n): the throwing or splashing of liquid against something

Dear Dash,

I will forever regret the decision I made to leave you, Kara, and Dad. It was a terrible mistake on my part, and I am so sorry for all the pain I brought you and the family. I hope that someday you can forgive me.

While I have no excuse to offer, I do want to explain how I made such a selfish choice. Dad and I fell in love at a young age. We soon married, and quickly had you, and then Kara. It all seemed to happen so fast. One day, I was a young girl, filled with dreams of travelling, having a career in music, and raising a wonderful family. The next moment, I was married with two young kids. I feared that the doors for my other dreams were closing for me, and I panicked. Dad and Grandpa tried patiently to help me develop a plan that would accomplish all these dreams, but I felt like I was losing my identity. That's when I left.

In retrospect, those days with you, Kara and Dad were the best days of my life. It took a journey of many heartbreaks for me to understand that I had all I ever wanted right at home with my family.

In the midst of pursuing my dreams, I stumbled across this book. The rabbit's story is similar to my own. He began his journey surrounded by love, but took it for granted, focused solely on his own interests. He then sets off on an adventure, in which his heart gets broken several times, but through that heartache, a miracle happens. He learns to recognize how much love is around him, and how to return that love to the people in his life. It is a miraculous journey.

I have had a similar journey, learning that the greatest gift I have in my life is my family. I hope you can forgive me. I love you.

Mom

Over the next couple hours, I laid in my bed and devoured that book, visualizing Mom as the rabbit, Edward, who became Susannah, then Malone, and Clyde, and Jangles, and finally back to Edward. I saw her, ignoring the love around her, getting her heart broken, and eventually learning to cherish the people in her life through the pain she suffered. I wanted for us to go back in time; to be a whole family again. I wanted her to be forgiven, but I didn't know how to forgive her.

It was a fitful night trying to sleep in room 207. I could hear Dad tossing around on the cot next to me, and remember him coming in and hour or so ago. It was long after I had closed my eyes. I think he had been reading for a while, because I sensed the sound of pages turning while I lay with my eyes closed trying to sort through my thoughts. At some point he must have dozed off, because I see the book that Paige gave him lying beneath his arm.

My body is so drained, but my mind is racing. I keep thinking about Mom, and her journey. All I ever thought about was how much she hurt me, and our family. Now I see how much she hurt herself. I can relate to her dreams. She wanted to make a name for herself. She wanted her life to matter. Maybe she figured out that it did matter, but that her dreams were fulfilled in a way different than she had imagined.

I also thought about Paige, and her courage. She seemed so content. She had so little, and yet gave so much. She had the ability to somehow touch the lives around her.

Wait a minute, the last time I saw her she called me 'Edward'. Edward?

Then it hit me.

This book wasn't just about Mom. It was my journey, too.

I had been surrounded by love, but was focused on my own interests. I had closed my own heart. I was afraid of being hurt, and in that fear, couldn't fully love the people around me. I had not only been heartbroken, but had broken hearts around me. I was Edward. And Clyde. And Jangles.

"Dad, are you awake?"

"What is it, son? Are you okay? Do you need me to get the Doctor?"

"No Dad, I need your phone. I need to call Mom."

It seems that it was a fitful night at home too, because Mom answered the phone on the first ring.

"Mom, it's Dash. Can you come early tomorrow morning?"

"Of course, Son. Are you all right?"

"Yes Mom. I just want to talk. And Mom...?" my voice caught.

"Yes, Dash?"

"I love you."

"I love you too Son!"

Dad didn't say anything, but his hand rubbing my back as I hung up his phone told me that he was proud of me.

Somewhere through the mental anguish that night, I had an epiphany. Paige was right - there was something that I needed to do, and now I see it. Instead focusing my remaining time doing something that will be remembered by others, I want to use my time to 'remember' the people who surround my life right now. I want to enjoy and cherish people in the moment.

I am going to alter the plans for the 5K race. Instead of focusing on raising awareness for Hodgkin's disease, I want the race to somehow be geared towards cherishing the people that are in our lives right now. While we waited for daylight and Mom's visit, I explained to Dad what I had been thinking.

I also want to set up some type of forum for students and seniors to interact. I have gained so much from my relationship with Grandpa, as well as my short time here with Stan and Mudge. It is also obvious that kids my age have a lot to offer today's seniors. There is no doubt that Paige enriched the seniors here, and vice-versa. After playing around with some ideas with Dad, we sketch out the framework for a club at school that will spend monthly time with some of the seniors at the facility. Their relationships will hopefully be a mutual benefit to one another. We tentatively have named it the "Extra Innings" Club.

Next, I got some tape and fixed the photo that I had torn weeks before, taping it inside the back cover of the book. Underneath I wrote - *Family: Even when we leave, we never stop loving. I love you all. Dash.* On the opposite page, I wrote Mom a short note.

After Mom texted Dad that she was on her way up the elevator, I ambled with my walker out to meet her. I couldn't believe it when I saw her, how beautiful she looked, bald, without a hat, and smiling to see me.

"Hey Mom! Thanks so much for coming so early today!"

"Of course, Dash!"

Dad offered to take Kara to the cafeteria so Mom and I could have a few minutes, but I said I wanted us all together. As a family. We slowly made our way back to 207, and though my body was feeling weaker by the day, I hadn't felt so invigorated in weeks.

"Mom, Dad, Kara - I just want to say I'm sorry. I'm so sorry for closing up my heart to you guys. For letting my own goals and ambitions come before our family. And for letting my hurt feelings harden my heart towards you all.

Dad, though we have been close, there are still times I just didn't want to listen to you. I'm so sorry.

Kara, I feel so ashamed for fighting with you, or complaining about you. You're a great sister and I am so lucky to have you in my life!

Mom, I'm so sorry for shutting you out these past several years. I let my hurt feelings get in the way of understanding you, and letting you be human. I love you and want you back in my life. Can you forgive me?"

We hugged and huddled for the rest of the day, watching family videos and perusing old photo albums. We were making up for lost time and missed moments. Paige was right. I knew what I wanted, and it wasn't so much to make a name for myself, but to enjoy my namesakes - my family. Over the course of that day I decided to use my remaining time not to worry about saying my "goodbyes", but rather focus on my "helloes", embracing the moments I had left. Paige may not have had the opportunity to choose how she died, but she certainly chose how to live, and I was going to follow suit. Whatever remained of my 'dash', the time between my own numbers, would be spent loving others and enjoying their love.

Chapter 14

dash — (idiom): to cut a dash, to make a striking impression

Due to my diminishing state and the constant need for pain medications, I had been relegated to living in the facility for the past several weeks. Convinced that there is nothing more that they can do, the hospital staff has decided to let me finish my remaining days at home with a hospice nurse living with us. They have moved a hospital bed into our family room, and set up the entire room for my family to camp around me.

Even Squirt is here, though Dad has had to clean up plenty of little messes since I have been back. I'm glad Squirt is so excited to see me. And Mom has been here around the clock, so it feels like she never left. I hope she moves back in with Dad and Kara.

But I'm not done yet. I still have a race to help organize. After a lot of brainstorming, we decided to make it a 2.62 mile 'micro-marathon'. This race will symbolize both the incredible endurance and wisdom that our seniors bring to the table, as well as the new, energetic perspective of the younger generation. I wanted to name it "The Extra-Innings Race", but Joey and my family submitted the paperwork to our town with the name "The Extra-Innings Dash". It was a tremendous honor.

Joey told me that Coach Fitz has recruited not only our entire cross country team, but the teams from several other schools across the county. Kara let me know that Stan and Mudge have worked to get seniors out to the race from several different facilities in the area. They are going to be cheering on the runners at the start / finish line. Stan said they consider it a road trip they are all looking forward to.

Our hope is that by bringing students and seniors together, we will begin to build a bridge between generations. Hopefully, students will begin to connect to all the wisdom and insight that the seniors have to offer. They can either serve as older mentors, or friends with listening ears. And the seniors can really benefit by seeing the value they still have to give. I saw the joy that both Stan and Mudge had whenever we visited them, their eyes lighting up and their spirits lifting up. Maybe we are on to something.

I haven't been out of the bed in three days, but I am hoping to have the strength to go to the race and toss out the ceremonial first pitch, which will be used like a starter's pistol to initiate the race on Saturday.

Dad and Kara went out to get pizza for the family. I really haven't eaten any normal food in the past week, because my stomach doesn't seem able to process the foods anymore. The nurse has been feeding me intravenously, which really sucks since Dad is bringing home a Hawaiian pizza from Vinnie's, my all-time favorite restaurant. I told him it would be ok, and that maybe I could just suck on a piece or two. I could always feed it to Squirt afterwards.

After dinner, Mom, Dad and Kara all gather on my bed.

"Sweetheart, we have a couple things for your big day this weekend." Mom says.

My nurse, Jan, wipes off my face so I can try to speak. I have been losing my voice the past few days, but I manage to squeak out a broken "What is it?"

First, Mom and Kara produce a shoe box. I don't have the strength to sit up and open it, so they do the honors for me. It is a pair of shiny black and silver racing flats.

"I know you're not able to run, but we want you to know that you've run a great race already." Mom says.

"We're so proud of you." Kara adds.

They set them on my lap and Kara places my hands on the shoes. They feel amazing. Smooth. Fast. As she turns the shoes around so I could see them from all sides, I notice an inscription on the back of each.

"What do they say?" I moan.

"Daring Adventure. From Helen Keller's quote. Grandpa's favorite" Kara replies.

"We wanted you to know that your decision to organize this race is a daring adventure. In fact, I think you're whole life is one. We are so proud of you, Dash" Mom cries.

Next, Dad opens a gift bag for me. He pulls out a brand new White Sox jersey. Then he turns it around, and brings it close to me so I can read the name on the back. Abbott.

"Thanks, Dad!" I barely manage to squeak. "I love it!"

Finally, Kara brings out my collection of autographed balls and sets them on a tray before me.

"Which one would you like to throw out to start this weekend's race?" she asks.

I hadn't really thought about that. I guess I had just pictured some random ball. But this is such a great idea. With my eyesight fading, I can't see the autographs clearly, but the vision of each ball is still clear in my memory. Which one should I use to commemorate the event? Should I use the first ball from my collection, the one with Jeter's autograph? What about the ball from my favorite player, Robin

Ventura? Or I could toss the one from Grandpa's all-time favorite player, Roberto Clemente.

It is an easy decision.

I raise my finger, motioning Kara to bend over so she can hear me.

"The Abbott ball." I whisper.

While I love all the balls in my collection, this is the ball from the last chapter fo my life. The other balls remind me of that quest I was on to accomplish something. They were the beginning of my race. This ball is the conclusion. It reminds me of the struggles that Paige and I endured. The other balls point to the men of character I aspired to be like. This ball reminds me of the challenges that forged character inside of me. I think Grandpa would agree.

Kara places the ball in my hand. The cover feels so soft, almost like a velvet robe. Yet I can tell the core is solid, like iron or steel. It reminds me of Paige. She was so gentle and kind, but had the strength of a champion. She was velvet over steel.

"Let me try to throw it." I groan.

"Wait, I'll be right back" Mom calls.

After a few moments, she returns, with a camera, and my mitt. The one she had given me all those years ago. The one I was wearing in that family photo that I tore up.

"Jan, would you mind taking a picture of us?" Mom asks.

"Of course."

Grabbing Squirt, Kara and Dad flank the sides of the bed. Mom sits next to me, wearing the mitt open as I hold up the ball. As I drop it in her mitt, Jan snaps a couple pictures.

"Steeerike!" Dad calls out.

We made it. We are a family once again. My wish has been granted.

Chapter 15

dash – (n): the reverberating sound of splashing heard from afar.

Though he didn't get to see it, the race was a success. Later that night that Jan had taken his picture tossing the 'first pitch' to me, Dash eventually crossed his own finish line. His race was done.

On Saturday, there was an outpouring of support for our family at the Extra Innings Dash. A couple hundred kids showed up from local schools, many with their heads shaved. Joey and Kara had designed shirts for all the participants with a picture of Dash and Paige on the front, and Helen Keller's 'daring adventure' quote on the back. A handful of students even offered to walk with the seniors, pushing some in their wheelchairs for the entire course. There was also a huge showing from community members, some of who walked, and others who ran.

Coach Fitz started the race with a brief speech, commemorating what an amazing athlete and team member Dash was, with a short video of some of my son's races from school playing behind him. He also had pulled some strings with some contacts in the local media, and the race wound up with coverage that night on a few of the television stations. The brief news story told the tale of my son, and his friend Paige, and their courage in battling Hodgkin's disease. The story also covered the endearing friendship they had forged with the seniors at the facility, the race, and the forming of the "Extra-Innings Project". On one channel, the newscaster even wore the race shirt as she told the story.

Stan and Mudge rustled up friends from the senior wing, and with the help of Joey and Kara they created hundreds of luminaria that lined both sides of the street leading into the finish line chute. The luminaria were made out of white paper lunch bags, that had glow sticks illuminated inside. On the outside of the bag, they punched various star-shaped holes to let the light shine out. Eventually, participants at the race purchased these bags, writing the name of a friend or loved one who had their own experience battling cancer. After the race, half of the bags were moved to the front walkway of the hospital facility where Dash, Paige and the seniors had met. The other half were used to line the front walkway to our house.

On Dash's last night home, I lay next to him on the bed, holding him in my arms, reading to him from *The Miraculous Journey of Edward Tulane*. I tried to keep him warm, and comfort him as he struggled against the pain raging within. I wanted to savor the moments that we had remaining. With my arms wrapped around him, I recalled memories of holding a younger Dash. Hugging him before bed, clutching him when he was afraid, embracing him when he needed a mother's love. For several years, I missed those hugs terribly. I yearned to hold my son. Despite the circumstances, I'm grateful that I was able to have that opportunity. In that moment, all I could do was hold him.

He thrashed violently for a while, then rested comfortably in my arms while I closed the book and told him a story. It was a story about two overlapping journeys. One journey belonged to a woman. She started in a happy home, surrounded by love, but secretly felt incomplete. She thought she needed something more. She felt that she had to accomplish something, maybe to be worthy of that love. Leaving her home on a mission to find this dream, she wound up losing all that she loved. The other journey was her sons, a talented youth who was also driven to accomplish something. To prove something. To be something.

Each of these journeys was filled with heartache, and eventually, heartbreak. But each of these heartaches produced the seeds of healing for both mother and son. Their heartbreaks contained the lessons that shaped their character. Along the journey, the mother's leaving never stopped her loving. The son's pain couldn't cover his desire to connect. In the end, they together accomplished a miracle that saw both journeys start, and finish, in the same home, reunited.

As Dash rested in my arms, I flipped open the book, and noticed the picture I had given him weeks before was taped inside the back cover, with a wonderful insight about our family's love beneath it. On the opposite page, Dash had left me a note.

Dear Mom,

I'm sorry to say that I avoided reading this book for some time. I'm also sorry for ripping the photo. I guess the title of this book reminded me of when Grandpa used to say that he believed you were on a "Miraculous Journey." I was too mad, and too hurt to believe it. I gave up on you, and on us. It was easier, and safer to just care about myself.

After meeting Paige I started to see things differently. She reminded me what truly mattered - the people in your life.

I thought this book would be about your journey, and assumed that is why you gave it to me. But after reading it, I realized that this book is really about my journey as well. I saw myself in Edward, and Malone, and Clyde and Jangles. And then I realized that I wanted my own miracle - for our family to be together again.

It doesn't matter to me anymore that you left. It only matters that you came back. Thank you for giving me my miracle. I love you, Mom.

Always your son,

Dash

For more information visit:

www.dashthebook.wordpress.com

www.dashthebook.com

or join the conversation about Dash on facebook, twitter, goodreads, or tumblr.

#dashthebook